I0545986

FreeForm Reborn

Saga of the Dandelion Expansion, Volume 2

Orrin Jason Bradford

Published by Porpoise Publishing, 2015.

Freeform Reborn
Orrin Jason Bradford

With the primary mission in jeopardy, the aftermath of its destruction threatens to tear one family apart...

With the brutal murder of his alien father, Homlin, still a vivid memory, young and impressionable TJ must undertake a journey of self-discovery in order to come to terms with the undeniable truth about his origins. The truth behind his alien heritage can no longer be denied, and the strange power of transformation that comes with it leads TJ down a path of realization and self-determination as he struggles to find his place in this world.

From the small town of Waynesboro, the effects of Homlin's primary mission ripple outwards into the world, carrying with it a promise of destruction and assimilation. Is the world safe from Homlin's true purpose? Is TJ just a dangerous pawn in his primary mission? Or has the battle for the fate of the Earth only just begun?Return now to Waynesboro at the turning of the tides. Join Pat, Allan, and TJ as they salvage the remains of their dysfunctional and unconventional family, and attempt to make sense of the awful reality that has come to alter their world.

Are You My Daddy?

1

"D addy," the young boy said, a look of confusion mixed with fear etched on his face as he stood at the mouth of the cave from which he'd just exited. Allan stared at him for a moment frozen in place.

"TJ?"

What in the world is he doing here? Allan wondered as he glanced around at the barren mountain landscape and the black abyss of the cave entrance.

Not your son. He heard Pat's voice reverberate through his mind and another part argue with her.

Yes, yes, it is my son. He looks just like Todd.

But you told me Todd was killed in the same house fire that took your wife years ago.

I know, but...but...but. Allan had no answer to that statement, for it was true. Allan shook himself back to the present and studied the boy in front of him.

Even though it had only been a day since he'd last seen the boy, he would have sworn TJ had grown at least another inch. *Probably my imagination,* Allan thought. *I know he's growing fast, but not that fast...right?* TJ looked to be between five and six years of age in appearance even though Allan knew his actual chronological age to be less than a year; more like six months. The FreeForm larva from which the boy had developed had amazing properties that Allan was still learning about.

"Daddy," TJ repeated, his voice wavering, a perplexed look on his young face. "She killed him. Why were they fighting?"

Allan glanced from TJ to the bloody half-man, half-catlike creature lying on the ground; all that remained of Homlin, the alien being that had started this whole mess; the alien being that had been instrumental in bringing FreeForm to the world and therefore indirectly TJ.

"He was a bad...man," Allan said, not quite knowing how to finish the sentence. "He hurt her and would have hurt a lot of other people as well."

"Does that make me bad as well?" TJ asked.

"No, of course not," Allan replied. "Why would you even think such a thing?"

"Well, I'm part him, aren't I? That's what he said."

Allan noticed the boy shiver then tilt his head to one side. Allan wasn't sure if TJ's shivering was from the frigid temperature that was continuing to drop as night approached, or from the question he had just asked.

Allan glanced at the large black wound on the side of the mountain once more and wondered for a moment what lay inside. This was a stark, isolated part of the North Carolina mountains; inhospitable, to say the least, and made even more so by the plunging temperatures and the slate gray sky that promised snow. Allan put down the tire iron Pat had asked him to retrieve and took off his jacket, offering it to the boy.

"Here, put this on. You're freezing."

TJ took the navy blue jacket and wrapped it around his shoulders. Clutching it in front of him, the windbreaker reached down to his ankles.

Allan reached out to him and started to pick him up, but TJ pulled away.

"Easy there. I'm not going to hurt you. We just need to get out of here before the snow comes."

"Home? Can we go home? See Kendra? Have Cheerios?"

"That's right," Allan said with a chuckle. "We're going home." Allan bent down to retrieve the tire iron before picking up his son. He strolled towards the helicopter where an injured Pat and an anxious Oliver waited.

2

IN THE DEEP RECESSES of the cave twenty or thirty yards from where Allan held the boy, a small ellipsoid-shaped globe the size of a large, slightly flattened grapefruit pulsated with a bluish purple glow. The anguished screams and the waves of the pain of the Primary had awakened the AI contained within it moments before. A high pitch whine reverberated from it throughout the cave and beyond, pricking the ears of several wild animals in the vicinity.

On the home planet, the Primary was known as Sluneg. The violent attack on Sluneg had caused the beta version of the Fail Safe Protocol to be initiated. The AI who referred to itself as Aeo struggled to manage the emergency and recover the consciousness of the Primary now known on this greenish-blue orb as Homlin. Unfortunately, the subject was in the final stages of dying, and nothing could be done to reverse the process. In use for the first time, the fail-safe mode had been designed for less intrusive, less violent, and less rapid cessation of the body that housed the Primary. In short, Homlin's consciousness was strung out all over the place and dissipating rapidly. Aeo struggled to pull all the pieces together and back into the cocoon for safe keeping.

Okay, I can do this, Aeo thought as it began the download process. *It's all out there. I just need to pull it together.* But the brain was dying rapidly, and the electrical signals that contained the information grew weaker by the second. Aeo finally had to admit that it would be unable to retrieve every part of the primary subject. It would have to make do with what it could recover and fill in the gaps later.

In the meantime, it scanned the cave and took inventory of the FreeForm available and was satisfied to find Homlin had stocked several in the pupal stage in the cave. *At least I'll be able to reconstruct another body for the Primary.* The Primary's mission could still be fulfilled. Aeo set to work to pick up the pieces of a mission that had gone bad.

Recovery

Allan pushed the door to Pat's hospital room open and stuck his head in. Glancing around, he was surprised to find her room looked more like a guest room you'd see in your favorite aunt's home. He then remembered reading in the Waynesboro's *Chronicle* that someone had willed a sizable amount of money to the institution expressly to rehab the rooms to be less sterile and more hospitable. *That had been money well spent*, Allan thought, as he noted the small flowered wallpaper that matched well with the bouquets of flowers that set on the chest of drawer and window seal.

Pat lay in bed with her head turned towards a window that looked out on the snow-covered courtyard. The snow had been falling for over eight hours. All details of the courtyard were entirely obscured, resembling mounds of cotton. Already the weather forecast stated it might be the worst storm to hit the southeast in over twenty years, with accumulations up to two feet. Even in Pat's four-wheel drive Cherokee, it had taken Allan close to a half hour to drive the ten miles from his home to the hospital, a drive that usually took no more than fifteen minutes. Travel was hampered in large part because of the Southern drivers without four-wheel drive who didn't have a clue how to maneuver in such conditions.

He noticed Pat had turned her head away from the window and was smiling weakly at him. He stood there smiling back as relief washed over him. Only then did he realize how afraid he had been of losing her.

"Are you just going to stand there gawking, or are you going to come over here and give me a kiss?" As she raised one hand to beckon him over, he noticed the attached I.V. drip. Her neck was bandaged from where the choker collar had cut into it. While she was still pale and weak, she looked better than when he'd last seen her in the helicopter the previous night. By the time he'd arrived at the helicopter, Pat had been securely strapped in by James, the pilot, and Oliver. Allan hadn't been able to tell if Pat had fallen asleep or had passed out, and he'd been too scared to ask. James and Oliver had stared at TJ with equally perplexed looks.

"What the hell happened?" Oliver asked. "Who's that?"

"I'll explain later," Allan promised, though he didn't have a clue what he'd tell them. "We've got to get her to a hospital."

Allan walked over to Pat's bed. His small bouquet of flowers looked puny next to the larger arrangements, but it had been the best he could do, considering the conditions outside where things continued deteriorating by the minute.

"Oh, they're lovely," Pat said as Allan bent over and kissed her. *Her color is better than last night*, he noted to himself, but her face was still missing its normally vibrant color. He could only imagine the hell she'd been through over the past twenty-four hours. Thankfully, it was finally over. Now they'd be able to get on with creating a life together without the concerns of an alien invasion.

Then again, there was TJ. How was he going to break the news to her about him? As far as he could tell, she'd been out of it last night and unaware of TJ's presence in the chopper. Maybe it would be better to wait until she was stronger, but even as he had the thought, he knew it was his way to put off an awkward conversation. So after a few minutes of pleasantries, he decided to broach the subject.

He started to sit in the straight back chair next to her bed, but Pat insisted he sit on the edge of the bed so she could see him better as well as hold his hand.

"What do you remember about the flight back to Waynesboro last night?" Allan finally asked.

"Not much, I'm afraid. Really nothing about the flight. The first thing I remember was waking up sometime in the middle of the night with one of the nurses checking my vitals. I could just make out the snow falling, and then I fell back into La-La land."

"I see," Allan said. "Well, I have some...some good news." At least, he considered it good news, and he hoped she would as well.

"Oh, good. I could use some good news right about now. What is it?"

"We found TJ last night. Actually, he found me. Isn't that great?" Allan held his breath as he studied Pat's face for a reaction.

Pat sat there. Her hand that had been gently rubbing his suddenly stopped. She stared at him, a startled look growing on her face.

"What?" she finally asked. "What did you say?"

"TJ. You know. He ran away a few days ago, and now he's back." He decided, given Pat's reaction, it might not help his case to let her know TJ had walked out of the cave where Pat and Homlin had fought to the death.

"And this is good news how?" Pat asked.

"He's alive," Allan answered, feeling the hackles on his neck rise. "My son is alive and well."

Pat slowly removed her hand from his and placed both of hers on her lap as she turned and stared out the window for close to a minute. Finally, she turned back to him.

"You've got to be kidding, Allan. He's not your son. He's not even human. He's as much an alien as the one I killed on that mountainside last night. We've got to let someone know about him."

Allan didn't know what to say in rebuttal, so he didn't say anything at first. He continued to stare at the woman he loved. How could he talk to her about how he felt about TJ when he wasn't sure himself? Part of him knew the boy wasn't his son, Todd, even though TJ was the spitting image of his son at that age. But Todd had come from his wife's womb in a normal pregnancy like everyone else on Earth...everyone but TJ. He had come from a late night C-section Allan had performed at his veterinary clinic back in March. At the time, he'd removed several larval looking fetuses from a stray dog that had taken up at the Parkers. Not knowing what to do with the strange creatures, he'd taken them to his home to observe. All the larvae had died in just a few days; all except the one that had slowly changed from looking like a premature puppy to his son. It had all happened by accident at first, and Allan had kept the larvae in the den. After all the other larvae had died, Allan had relocated the lone survivor to his son's old bedroom, surrounded by baby pictures of Todd. Over a few days, the larva went from resembling a puppy to looking like a small human baby. Allan had planned to contact someone in the government about what he had found, but he just couldn't bring himself to do it. He had to see what the larva was turning into.

And in the process, Allan had grown to love the boy he now called TJ. However, he also loved the woman lying in the hospital bed in front of him. Pat had almost been killed for a second time by an alien that had secretly been trying to take over the world and who had been the source of those larvae that Allan had removed from the Parker's stray dog.

Allan rose from the side of the bed and walked over to the window where he stared out at the falling snow. He'd always found snowstorms peaceful and calming, even severe ones like this that would wreak havoc on the area for several days. It seemed like a blanket of snow made everything less noisy, as though it absorbed much of the extraneous noises of life.

He'd probably been standing at the window for a good five minutes or more when he heard someone behind him clear their throat and a nurse say, "Visiting hours are over in five minutes, Dr. Allan."

He turned around and tried to smile back at her. "Thank you."

After the nurse left, Allan walked back to Pat's bed. He reached out with one hand and took hers. Finally, he said, "Can we agree not to do anything about this for at least a couple days? Let's get you back on your feet and home. Then we'll sit down and decide the best course of action. Okay?"

He could hear the pleading tone in that last word and hated himself for it but was relieved when he felt Pat squeeze his hand and nod before replying, "Where is he now?"

"Oh, he's at my house. Kendra came over last night before the storm became too bad. She's looking after him."

"I see," Pat said. "And what are you going to tell her? Are you going to keep lying to her as well?"

Once again Allan didn't know how to answer the question, so he just shrugged. "We'll have to sort that out as well."

Snowstorm

1

Twenty-four hours had passed since the Fail Safe Protocol had been initiated and its initial recovery task completed. Overall, Aeo assessed that the Protocol had performed well, considering the less than ideal circumstances and the fact that it had never been used before. Still, significant portions of Homlin's long-term memory had been lost. While it would be possible to re-install the Primary's mission into the subject's consciousness, most of the details of the last ten years that Homlin had been on the planet were either a jumbled mess or lost forever.

On the positive side of things, a significant early-in-the-season snowstorm had blanketed the area with close to two feet of snow, efficiently keeping anyone from investigating the area anytime soon. Also, during its efforts at gathering up the scattered pieces of Homlin's consciousness, Aeo had discovered the planet's inhabitants had invented a world wide web of information they referred to as the internet. Evidently, this species of Homo sapien wasn't as primitive as Aeo had initially thought. It felt certain this discovery would prove useful in recovering from this unexpected breakdown.

Unfortunately, that was about all the good news Aeo could come up with. It also had discovered that during the night while it had been concentrating on other matters, a pack of wolves had dragged Homlin's dead body away, leaving it up to Aeo to orchestrate the formation of a new body from scratch.

2

THE SNOWSTORM HAD DUMPED over two feet of snow through much of the North Carolina mountains, leaving thousands without power and even more stranded in their homes. Fortunately for Allan, he had prepared for such contingencies since he knew he'd have to be able to get to his veterinary clinic no matter what the weather. He had also spent years after veterinary school in New England where he also learned to drive in winter weather conditions. He even had two generators, one in his veterinary hospital and the other at home, just in case. Fortunately, neither area was affected by the power outage.

Upon arriving home with Pat around 3 PM, he found Kendra had put TJ down for his afternoon nap and had already called her mother to come pick her up from the main road near Allan's home. Allan had hoped to persuade her to stay as a way to avoid further conversations with Pat about TJ.

"I'm sorry, Dr. Allan, but I have homework to finish before tomorrow in case they call school back into session," Kendra said as she finished putting on her boots. "Besides, I'm sure you two need some time alone."

After Kendra left, Allan fidgeted around the house, fixing a fresh pot of coffee. He walked into the living room to stoke the fire in the woodstove while Pat made a nest of blankets and pillows in front of the stove. Allan fixed a tray with piping hot mugs of coffee and a pint of Kahlúa and placed it on the coffee table next to Pat. The two of them sat there for several minutes sipping on the spiked coffee and warming themselves. Finally, Allan placed his coffee mug back on the tray and turned to Pat.

"It's so good to have you back home," Allan said as he reached over and took Pat's hand." I don't know what I would have done if something had happened to you. I can only imagine what these last few days have been like for you, but I want you to know I love you very much."

Pat smiled and placed her other hand over top of his. "I love you too, Allan, and you're right. It was a harrowing experience, but it's over now."

The two of them sat there for several more minutes, enjoying the warmth of the fire. Finally, Allan turned back to Pat. "I know this may be hard for you to understand, but I want you to know that little boy sleeping in the next room is also important to me. Strange as it may sound, I've grown to love him. I believe, given some time, you could learn to love him as well."

Allan felt Pat stiffen as she pulled her hands away. "All I'm asking is for you to give it time," Allan hated the pleading tone creeping into his voice. "Give TJ and me time. Will you do that?"

Pat turned and stared out the picture glass window to the winter scape. Finally, with a broad sigh, she turned back to Allan. "I know when you look at TJ, you see a young boy that reminds you of your deceased son. Somehow you've taken the leap and convinced yourself that's who he is, but when I look at him, I'm reminded of an alien that almost killed me on two different occasions. I don't see a young, innocent boy. I see a threat to this planet and to humanity. I know, Allan, that you care for him, but I don't think I will ever be able to see him as anything other than what he is."

"I understand," Allan finally replied, "but for me and for the future we could share together, would you be willing to try?"

Pat stared at her hands in her lap. She reached for the pint of Kahlúa and poured several ounces of the liqueur into her coffee mug before taking a couple deep swallows.

"I don't know how to answer that question. I'll need at least a day or two to think it over. In the meantime, I need to get drunk. Do you have anything stronger in the house?"

Suds and Duds

James Stepp walked into the Suds and Duds for the first time in over four years. The unlikely combination pub and laundromat had been a favorite hangout of his when it first opened. Everyone had predicted it would never make it, especially in a town as small as Black Mountain, but it had turned out to be surprisingly successful. Now, James was returning to his old digs for a drink as a way of acknowledging the dramatic changes that had taken place over the past four years.

As James ordered a Jack and Ginger from a bartender he didn't recognize, he reflected on the last time he'd been in the bar just before his life had performed a triple somersault off the high dive. He had become a regular at the Suds and Duds so he could tell his wife, Jenny, he was helping out at home by doing the laundry. He figured it was the least he could do to help her out since she'd not been feeling well of late. It was also an excellent excuse to get out of the house and chill out at the bar and flirt with Marjorie, the barkeep. He prayed Jenny wouldn't ask him about the washer and dryer in their basement. If she did, he would have to explain to her that both appliances had been broken for months, but he would cross that bridge when he came to it.

He picked up his beer and downed half of it before swiveling around in his seat to stare at Marjorie waiting on another regular at the other end. He figured Marjorie to be between forty-five and fifty. Despite spending most of her time managing the two businesses, she somehow kept herself in shape. Besides, James had a strange attraction for women who wore their long hair in a ponytail. That's what had attracted him to Jenny more years ago than he liked to admit; that along with her killer body and sexy, Southern accent. But his wife seldom wore her hair in a ponytail these days, and her body had gone from sexy to Rubenesque to pudgy. Still, late at night with the lights off, her Southern drawl could still excite him.

I really don't need to be ogling other women, James thought as he took another gulp of his beer. After all, he was a married man with a two-year-old daughter and a second one on the way. Still, it was hard not to look, especially when you were married to a woman who was always too tired to pay attention to him and was rapidly growing into a... Best not to finish that thought, James told himself as he caught Marjorie's attention and motioned for another beer.

"Here you go, suugarrr," Marjorie said as she set a fresh beer in front of him. "You look kind of down tonight. What's up?"

"Oh, nothing," James replied, pushing the empty mug towards her and picking up the fresh one. "It's just that I'm, well...bored. I mean, I know I'm not a big city sort of a guy. I've spent most of my life in small towns because that's what I prefer, but sometimes I'd like something interesting to happen."

"Tell me about it, sweetie," Marjorie replied as she wiped the bar with a moist towel. "But remember, be careful what you ask for. You might find that boredom is better than the alternative."

"Yeah, you're probably right," James said as he rubbed the frost off the side of his mug.

As Marjorie went to wait on another customer, James continued to sit at the bar and reflect upon his life. He hadn't realized until that evening just how bored he'd become. His heating and air conditioning business barely paid the bills, and even in the busy season, it bored him. Funny thing, the happiest he could remember being was when he was in the service, especially while overseas fighting for liberty, justice, and the American way. There was something about an army of other soldiers trying to kill you in oh so many different ways that brought a certain freshness and edge to life.

Then there was the thrill and exhilaration he experienced flying. He relished the feel of landing a group of soldiers in a hot war zone, the yelling of the men, the sound of gunfire and explosions all around him and knowing it was fate, not skill, that kept him alive. Man, what a rush. God, he missed that. Oh, he took the occasional trip out to the local airfield, and that helped, but flying a Cessna 172 was hardly the same as flying a Black Hawk or even a Huey, especially while soldiers on the ground were trying to knock you out of the sky.

Yep, his life had grown pretty dull in the last few years, but what could he do about it? There were those occasional calls he'd receive from an old Army buddy or two who had leveraged their training as Green Berets into lucrative careers as soldiers of fortune, but each time he had been contacted, he begged off. That was hardly the life for a married man with children.

What was that Marjorie had just said? "Be careful what you ask for. You might find what you have is better than the alternative," or something like that. *Maybe she's right*, James thought. *Maybe I should be satisfied with what I've got.*

James finished off the Jack and Ginger and caught the eye of the bartender to order another one. Funny how one's perspective on life often changed over time. Boredom looked pretty attractive these days.

Bona Fide Genius

1

TJ sat in the middle of the great room of Allan's ranch style log home. Besides his bedroom, it was TJ's favorite part of the house, not only because it was the warmest location, but also because of the large window that provided a panoramic view of the outdoors with its mix of evergreens, hardwood trees, and thick underbrush. That's where TJ really wanted to be, but Kendra and he had already taken a long walk through the newly fallen snow. Kendra had finally insisted they return home so she could fix them both some hot chocolate.

TJ sat cross-legged on the rug, surrounded by walls of multi-colored Legos behind which he hid an army of toy soldiers. He pretended to play, but as soon as Kendra walked into the kitchen to fix the hot chocolate, he scampered up. He ran into the spare bedroom Allan had recently converted into a home office. There, sitting on the desk, was the toy TJ really wanted to play with. His dad had called it an iMac computer and had brought it home from work. None of that made much sense to TJ, who was far more fascinated by the beautiful pictures that magically appeared on the computer screen whenever the computer was left alone for several minutes.

After watching the pictures rotate for a minute or two, TJ climbed onto Allan's office chair to get a better look. He knew he might get in trouble for messing with the computer, but he just couldn't resist. He soon discovered he could just reach the flat plastic slab and smaller object that sat in front of the screen. He'd seen his dad playing with those and knew they were somehow connected to the rest of the iMac. It didn't take long for his youthful curiosity to get the better of him. He reached out and grasped the small, rounded object as he'd seen Allan do. Immediately, the pictures disappeared.

Next, TJ discovered the small object in his right hand controlled a small arrow that glided across the screen. He played with the arrow for a couple of minutes, pretending it was a bird under his command. This led him to the pretty pictures that popped up at the bottom of the screen when he directed the arrow in that direction. He continued to experiment, this time with the button on top of the object in his hand. His next significant breakthrough came when he discovered that if he quickly clicked the button twice while the arrow hovered over one of the small images, much like he'd noticed Allan had done, larger pictures appeared.

He was concentrating on the new pictures so intently that he never noticed when Kendra walked into the room carrying a tray with two steaming mugs of hot chocolate and a large bowl of Cheerios.

"There you are, you little rascal," she said. "I was looking all over the place for you. Didn't you hear me calling you?"

TJ shook his head without taking his eyes off the screen. 'Uh-uh," he mumbled. He twisted his tongue between his lips as he concentrated on his efforts.

"Oh my, you mustn't play with Dr. Allan's computer," she said as she placed the tray on the desk and pulled the chair TJ was sitting on away so he could no longer reach the machine. "He'd kill me if anything were to happen to it."

She pulled the chair closer to the desk to make it easier for TJ to reach the bowl of Cheerios. "Now you have to promise not to snitch on me to Dr. Allan about what you're having for lunch. Okay?"

"Snitch?" TJ asked as he took a handful of his favorite food and popped one of the tasty morsels in his mouth.

"Yeah, you know. Tell on me," Kendra replied, taking several of the Cheerios and plopping them into her cup where they floated like small life preservers in a sea of creamy chocolate.

After a couple of minutes, Kendra glanced over at the computer screen, then stared at it more intently. "What the..."

She turned to TJ. "Did you do that?" she asked, pointing to the picture TJ had drawn. It was a beautiful rendition of the view outside the great room's window.

Her tone frightened TJ at first. He shook his head and was about to deny he'd had any part in it, but then remembered his dad's lengthy talk at dinner a night or two ago about the importance of being honest. He changed his head shake into a nod.

"I didn't hurt anything."

"No, dear, I'm sure you didn't," Kendra said as she reached out and caressed his cheek. "It's very pretty. Let's save it so we can show your father."

TJ watched as she touched several areas of the plastic slab.

"You know how to use the...the..."

"It's called a computer, and yes, we have several of them at school, but I'm still learning. Maybe we can learn how to use it together. Would you like that?"

"Sure," TJ said, smiling broadly. Anything would be better than playing with those dumb blocks.

2

LATER IN THE AFTERNOON, Kendra sat TJ in front of the TV and inserted a DVD into the player. "How about watching *The Lion King* for a bit while I make a call?"

"Okay," TJ agreed. He found the movie a bit simple, but he liked how it ended. Besides, he often had more fun listening in on other people's conversations while they thought he was either sleeping or watching television.

After the movie had started, Kendra walked over to her purse and pulled out her cell phone, then returned to the couch where she curled up with one of the comforters before placing her call.

TJ twisted around on the floor so he could see the television and also keep one eye on Kendra. It felt good to be home where it was warm and dry and where there was an unlimited supply of Cheerios. He especially liked Kendra, who he thought of as part of his family, or at least a very close friend; a bit like Timon and Pumbaa. No, that wasn't exactly true. He knew his dad expected him to pay attention to Kendra and do what she asked. Maybe she was more like Sarabi, Simba's mother, but that didn't feel right either. *I don't have a mother, at least not like Simba.*

While Kendra was the one who primarily took care of him, Pat was the person closest to his dad, but no way could she be his mother. She didn't even like him. He'd overheard several heated conversations over the past few days. While he hadn't been able to make out all the words, he'd gotten the gist of them all. On top of that, hadn't she been the one who'd killed Homlin, his almost dad? Relationships were a most confusing part of life, but one thing was certain. Pat was no friend. To him, it felt like she was more like Scar than anyone else in the movie.

"Hello, Mimi? This is Kendra. Gotta minute?" TJ turned his attention and thoughts away from the movie and over to Kendra's phone conversation.

"I have some really great news. I'm not supposed to tell anyone, but I think I'll explode if I don't tell someone, but you've got to promise not to tell another soul. Promise? Your hand on a stack of Bibles promise?"

"Okay, good. Remember I told you I'd had a babysitting job that had ended? Yeah, that's the one. Well, it's back on. Yeah, I know, the money's great but here's the best part. Are you ready? My little boy...the one I'm sitting...he's a genius."

"No, really; a bona fide genius."

Rembrandt, Picasso, Van Gogh

1

When Allan returned home that evening from his veterinary clinic, Kendra pulled up the picture that TJ had created on the computer and showed it to him.

Allan stared at the picture for several seconds, then glanced first to Kendra and then through the doorway into the next room where TJ was once again pretending to play with his blocks and stuffed animals.

"You're pulling my leg, aren't you?" he asked Kendra.

It seemed like a strange comment to TJ since he couldn't imagine Kendra ever trying to pull his dad's leg or any other part of him for that matter. Perhaps it had another meaning that he didn't yet understand.

"No, promise, I'm not kidding you at all," Kendra replied. *Ahh, good,* TJ thought. Pulling one's leg means kidding someone. He'd be sure to remember that one.

"I left him right where he is now in the other room with his toys while I fixed lunch." TJ noticed that Kendra avoided revealing what they'd had for lunch. Apparently, she didn't want to snitch on herself.

"When I called him to eat, he didn't answer me, so I went to look for him. I found him in here, sitting in that chair. You'd evidently left the computer on this morning when you left for work. I'm guessing the screensaver caught his attention."

"How?"

TJ glanced up from stacking blocks to see his dad leaning over with his hands on the desk, staring intently at the computer screen.

"I don't know exactly," Kendra replied. "I wasn't here while he did it, but well..." She paused as though having trouble coming up with the right words. "At first I thought maybe you had done it and he'd just found it..."

"But you knew I couldn't draw something this beautiful," Allan finished for her.

"I've seen you try to sketch things when you're showing something to one of your clients. I know these iMacs are pretty neat, but...no, I was pretty sure you weren't the artist."

"Thanks a lot, but you're right," Allan said and chuckled. "There's no way I could have done this picture. Hell, I didn't even realize I had a graphics program on this thing."

"It appears that TJ is very smart," Kendra replied. "Like maybe even a genius."

Okay, TJ thought. *Genius equals very smart. Yeah, that's me, right? So why do you keep sticking me down here with these dumb blocks?* He watched as Allan walked in and out of his view, pacing back and forth in the office.

"I think you're right, Kendra," Allan finally said. "I can't wait to tell Pat tonight. Can you stay a little later in case she has questions? Join us for dinner?"

"Sure," Kendra replied. "I'll just need to let my mom know. I'd love to see Pat's face when you tell her."

TJ wasn't so sure Pat would be all that thrilled with the news.

2

THE FOUR OF THEM SAT around the table at the end of the meal. One lone piece of pizza lay on the pan, slowly turning into cardboard. Allan filled Pat's and his glass with Chianti while Kendra refreshed TJ's and her glass of grape juice. Allan had tried to create a celebratory mood all evening, but each time he tried, it fell flat. It didn't take a genius to know that something strange was going on between the two adults, and TJ was pretty sure he knew what it was—it was him. Pat tried to be cordial, but he'd noticed every time she glanced in his direction she'd quickly turn away and pick up her wine glass to take another swallow. He figured she'd easily finished over two-thirds of the bottle even though she'd only eaten one slice of pizza.

It appeared the wine was beginning to take effect as her eyelids drooped just a bit and the few times she'd attempted to join the conversation she'd slurred a couple of her words.

"I asked Kendra to stay for dinner tonight because we have something we wanted to share with you," Allan said as he picked up his glass and tipped it in Pat's direction. He opened the manila folder lying next to his plate and handed a copy of TJ's picture to her.

"What's this?" Pat asked after studying it for a moment.

"What does it look like?" Allan asked back.

"It looks like a computer-generated picture, a nicely rendered one." She glanced from Allan to Kendra and back to Allan. "Who did it?" she asked, then tried to answer her own question. "Musta been you, Kendra. I know Allan hasn't an artistic bone in his body."

"Ouch," Allan said. "Truth hurts sometimes, but you're right. I didn't do it, but neither did Kendra." He paused for dramatic effect.

"O...kay," Pat said as she placed the picture down on the table and picked up her wine glass and took a long swallow. "Again, my question. Who did it?" TJ could detect an edge of agitation growing in her voice.

"Guess," Allan replied, apparently unaware how annoying his little guessing game was to his partner.

"Rembrandt, Picasso, Van fucking Gogh," Pat all but screamed, then realizing she was overreacting, she said in a softer, more controlled voice. "I really don't know, and I'm sorry, but I'm not in the mood for your antics. Please, just tell me."

There was a long pause as Allan stared at Pat, a shocked look on his face.

"TJ did it this afternoon," Kendra finally said to break the strained silence.

Kendra and Allan had paraded around the house most of the early evening with the printed picture in hand, praising TJ for his artistic talent. TJ hadn't expected such an outburst from Pat but neither did he expect what came next.

Pat stared at the picture for a long moment, then turned her gaze in his direction. "You did this?" she asked, slowly nodding towards the picture.

"Yes, ma'am," TJ replied, smiling despite himself, but the smile quickly disappeared as he recognized the look of fear and distrust growing on Pat's face. She opened her mouth, about to say something, when her cell phone rang. She paused for a moment, then took the phone out of the pocket of her slacks. She glanced at the phone, a confused look replacing the fear.

"That's strange. It's my mother. She never calls me unless...Sorry, I have to take this," she said as she placed the phone to her ear.

"Hello, Mother. To what do I owe..." She stopped and listened to the person on the other end, a look of anguish growing on her face. She continued to listen for several seconds before finally saying, "Yes, I'll leave at once and catch the first plane that'll get me there. Try not to worry. He's a strong old goat."

She ended the call and dropped the phone on the now forgotten picture. "It's my dad. He had a massive heart attack earlier this evening. He's in intensive care. I've got to go to him."

"Of course," Allan said as he leaped out of his chair and went to her side. "I'll drive you to the airport. Kendra, will you call and see when the next flight to..."

"Alexandria," Pat finished for him. "I can fly into either Ronald Reagan or Dulles International."

TJ noticed her eyes tearing up. *So she has a dad who she loves as well,* he thought. Maybe she wasn't so bad after all.

"Also, Kendra, could you possibly stay and watch over TJ? I know it's a school night..."

"Don't worry about that. I have my books here. I'll call my mom and let her know. You two get yourself to the airport. I'll call you when I have the airline information."

"Thanks, Kendra," Allan said as he helped Pat from her chair. She wobbled a bit, but it was hard to tell if it was from the wine or the tragic news she'd just received.

As everyone rushed out of the kitchen, TJ remained in his chair, gazing down at the picture he'd drawn. His mind wasn't on the drawing but on the look he'd seen on Pat's face just before the phone call.

Fathers

1

While the main roads had finally been cleared of snow, many of the secondary roads were still covered in a hard packed mixture of ice and snow making driving hazardous for even the most expert driver. Usually, the journey to the Asheville airport could be covered in thirty to forty minutes. Tonight it would take nearly twice as long.

Kendra had called them with the airline schedule. The only remaining flight was due to leave in a couple hours on the way to Charlotte where Pat could catch another flight to Dulles. It would be tight, but they could make it...just.

The moonless night limited Allan's visibility. The wet blacktop of the recently cleared highway devoured the headlights, complicated by clumps of snow that kept falling from overhanging trees onto the SUV's windshield, mixing with the muddy spray from the cars in front of them. The tension that had concentrated along Allan's neck and shoulders was nothing compared to the strain inside the cab from the deathly silence.

Allan knew how close Pat and her father were. She often referred to him and more than once he'd heard them joking with each other on the phone. *She must be worried to death,* Allan thought as he flipped on the windshield wipers to clear the snow and moisture, only to spread it into an icy mess.

"I had a thought during dinner." Allan finally broke the silence. "Want to hear it?"

"I guess," Pat replied unenthusiastically.

"I think it's time we enroll TJ in school. Clearly, he's smart enough to handle it. I wouldn't be surprised if he made the honor club, though I guess they don't have that until they get a little older."

There followed a long pause. Allan thought Pat hadn't heard what he'd said and started to repeat it when she replied.

"You're kidding, right?" The condescending tone of her voice was unmistakable.

"I don't know. It's been a few years since I was involved with school. They might have some kind of honor thing..."

"That's not what I'm talking about," Pat interrupted. "You can't be serious about enrolling TJ into school."

"Why not?" Allan replied. "You know he's smart enough. The picture proves that not to mention how curious and interested he is in learning."

"Let me ask you a question," Pat said with just a little less edge. "How old is TJ?"

"I'd say he'd pass for five easily. Probably even six or seven."

"No, that's how old he looks, but how old is he actually? How long has he been alive?"

Allan thought about the questions and suddenly realized where Pat was going with her question. "Oh, yeah, I guess we'd have to work around that somehow."

"What? Like changing schools every few weeks because he's obviously growing so fast that no one could help but notice?" Pat said with such sarcasm that Allan could feel his hackles raise. "And there's at least one other little matter you'd have to 'work around.'"

"What's that?" Allan finally asked though he was pretty sure he wasn't going to like the answer.

"He's an alien!" Pat shouted.

"Oh, we're not going to start that again, are we?" Allan shot back.

"Start it again? No, because we never ended it in the first place. You asked me to give it some time. Well, I have, and yet nothing has changed. That thing back there you call TJ is still not of this world. You're still refusing to deal with reality, and I'm still unwilling to live in your fantasy world where deceased boys come back to complete the happily ever after fairy tale."

Allan suddenly swerved the car to avoid a tree limb that had fallen onto the edge of the road. He fought to bring the SUV back under control. When he finally did, he turned and glanced at Pat.

"Why don't you tell me how you really feel?"

"Good try, but humor isn't going to work here," Pat replied a little calmer. "It's not going to have this issue magically disappear. It's going to need to be dealt with. You even thinking for a moment about enrolling TJ into school demonstrates how out of touch with reality you are. Maybe it's a good thing I'm being called away right now. I think we could use a little break. Our lives have certainly been overwhelming lately."

Allan could feel Pat staring at him even though she appeared as only a silhouette in the dark cab. She sighed. "I really can't deal with this tonight though. Just get me to the airport and, after this crisis with my dad is over, we'll talk. Until then, how about a truce?"

"Yeah," Allan replied. "Fair enough."

2

PAT STROLLED DOWN THE hallway of the Inova Alexandria Hospital on the way to ICU. The determined look on her face was matched by the gait of her walk.

I swear if one more nurse or orderly asks me where I'm going, I'm going to punch them out, she thought as she rounded the corner and saw a sign for her destination. A kind, matronly nurse looked up from her paperwork has Pat approached and gave her a warm smile.

"Good morning, dear," the nurse said as she stood up and walked around the counter. "You must be Pat."

"That's correct," Pat replied, momentarily taken aback." How did you know my name?"

"From your father. He described you right down to your walk," the nurse replied with a chuckle. "He warned me that if I tried to stop you from seeing him, I would be taking my life in jeopardy. So if you would please come with me, he's waiting to see you."

As of two of them walked through a set of swinging double doors, the nurse said, "We have a dumb rule here of no visitors in ICU, but since you are family if we keep this discreet it shouldn't be a problem. Besides, the older I get, the more I seem to enjoy bending or even breaking such stupid rules."

She pointed to a door they were approaching. "He's right in there."

Pat thanked her and slowly pushed the door open, suddenly frightened by what she might see on the other side. Her father lay propped up in bed with a myriad of tubes and wires running from him that included an IV in his left arm and a small tube running up his nose to supply him with oxygen. Pat could hear a rhythmic *beep beep* that matched the squiggly lines on one of the monitors. Her father's face was turned towards the door. Pat was alarmed to see that his normally vibrant tan complexion had been replaced with a gray pasty mask.

As she walked into the room, her father's eyes fluttered open, and he smiled weakly. "I hope this doesn't mean that the hospital is going to have to replace its ICU head nurse."

"No, she heeded your warning," Pat replied and laughed. It was good to see that her father still had his sense of humor.

"Come over here where I can see you," her father said in a voice just slightly above a whisper. "And don't mind all these wires and tubes. I'm thinking of auditioning for a part in one of those hospital shows on TV."

Pat rushed to him, jumping on his chest to give him a big hug. Realizing what she had done, she pulled back.

"Oh, I'm sorry!"

"No need to apologize, my dear," her father replied." I'm sure if my doctor were here he would prescribe a big hug from my daughter. It's exactly what I need right now."

Pat gave him a second hug but more gently this time. Seeing him like this, she realized how much he meant to her and how much she had missed him. Oh sure, they spoke on the phone every couple of weeks, but it wasn't the same as being face-to-face. In years past, she had rationalized not visiting more often by telling herself she was just too busy. She had her business as a private investigator to manage, and of course, in this past year, there'd been the small matter of stopping an alien from taking over the world. The thought reminded her of the argument she had had with Allan just a few hours ago. Could his relationship with TJ be anything like the relationship she and her father shared? After all, in Allan's world, TJ was the son who he loved dearly and would do anything for. Was that really all that different? Yes, came the answer. *I am the product of a union between two humans. TJ is not.*

"You know, dear, I'm going to be fine," her father said as he gently rubbed her hair.

His words brought her back to the present, and she stood up. She put her hand to her face to rub an itch and was surprised to find it come away wet with tears, a response she hadn't had in a long time. When she had gotten the call about her father's condition, it had scared her more than anything else she'd experienced over this past year, and that had been a lot. For her entire life, her father had been her staunchest supporter through thick and thin, never giving up on her and always finding the positive even in the darkest of times. *Just like Allan is there for TJ* flashed in her mind, and was immediately refuted with a loud *no, it's not the same.*

Pat sat on the edge of the bed, careful not to disturb any of the tubes and wires. She reached out and grasped her father's hand, surprised by its coolness. She studied his hand and was surprised once again. She had always known her father to have the strongest hands of anyone she'd ever met, but the ones she now looked at were those of an old man. Where had those age marks come from, and when had the skin become paper thin? When had all that changed? When had her father grown old?

Little Helpers

1

The following afternoon Allan made it a point to leave the office a little early so he would have time to talk to Kendra about enrolling TJ into school. When he opened the door and walked into the great room, he noticed Kendra in the midst of transforming the room into a Christmas Wonderland. She was arranging a garland around a metal frame. Several boxes of Christmas decorations sat on the floor, waiting to be unpacked. Allan glanced around to find TJ dressed in a forest green outfit complete with a Santa Claus hat and shoes with turned up toes. "Well, TJ, aren't you something? I don't know what exactly but something," he exclaimed.

"He's Santa's little helper," Kendra said as she turned around and walked over to Allan. Then in a softer voice, she said, "Someone had to introduce him to the Christmas season. Besides, my mom isn't all that into Christmas these days, so I didn't want these decorations to go to waste. I hope it's okay with you."

"Sure, I guess. It's fine. No, more than fine. It's a great idea. I've had my mind on so many other things. In fact, that's why I'm home early. I want to run an idea by you."

"Okay," Kendra replied. "Is it alright if TJ and I continue to decorate while you talk?"

"Yes. I may even help you," Allan replied as he opened one of the boxes and looked inside. "While I may have missed introducing TJ to the Christmas season, I have been thinking about other aspects of his education." Allan paused for a moment, then dove into his well-prepared speech intended to convince Kendra into helping him with the idea. He continued to lay out his plans, including the conversation he had had with Pat on the way to the airport, leaving out the details of why Pat was opposed to his idea.

"So you see, Kendra, I'm going to need your help with this plan. I thought we would wait until after school starts back in session the first of the year. It might be a good idea for TJ to take a placement test to see which grade to start him in. What do you think of my idea?"

Kendra put down the string of lights she was untangling and glanced over to TJ. "Honey, could you give your father and me a minute alone? Why don't you take that box of decorations there to your room and decorate it?"

TJ did as he was told and after he had left, Kendra turned back to Allan. She picked up the lights again and fidgeted with them for a minute before finally looking directly at Allan. "I'm afraid, in this instance, I have to agree with Pat."

"You what?"

"Pat is right. It would be a really bad idea to enroll TJ in school and here's why. You and I know TJ is an extraordinary little boy, but unfortunately children his age won't see him as special. They will only see him as strange, weird, different, and kids can be very cruel when they want to be. I'm afraid TJ would be taunted and bullied."

Allan slowly nodded. "I hadn't thought about that," he admitted.

"However," Kendra continued, "I agree with you that TJ needs an education, and there is more than one way for a smart boy like him to be educated."

"What did you have in mind?" Allan asked.

"We could homeschool him," Kendra said smiling broadly. "It's really a perfect solution. I've been thinking seriously about going into teaching after I graduate in a couple of years and my helping with TJ's homeschooling would be perfect training for me. I've been doing some research on the internet while at school and there are a lot of resources available for homeschooling families and more coming online every day."

"Homeschool him? I have to admit I don't know much about what's involved in homeschooling, but it sounds interesting and probably much more practical for TJ, given his special situation."

"Speaking of which," Kendra added. "While I was on the internet, I did some additional research about conditions that result in rapid growth among children, but I couldn't find anything that would cause the rate of growth that I've witnessed in TJ."

"Like I said, his condition is quite rare and..."

Kendra held up her hand to stop him. "You don't have to say anything else, Dr. Allan. I know you're just trying to protect him, but you don't need to protect him from me. I don't know what's going on here with TJ and, to tell you the truth, I don't need to know. You see, I love that little guy as though he were my own. There's nothing I wouldn't do for him, and that includes protecting him from those little monsters that he would run into in a public school. So can we agree that homeschooling is the best route to go?"

Allan nodded, walked over, and gave Kendra a big hug.

2

IT WAS TIME FOR AEO to proceed with the process of reconstructing a body for the consciousness formally known as Homlin. For that, it would use a pupal stage of the FreeForm and a surrogate. Aeo just needed to select the best pupa to grow the body, but what animal could it find to implant the pupae in for gestation? It started by analyzing the skeletal remains of the large animal it had found in the cave and determined it to be a black bear. Another of this species should do nicely as a surrogate.

While such a surrogate could be either female or male in a pinch, the process was simpler in a female so Aeo went about formulating pheromones that would attract a fully grown female. It took only a couple of days before Aeo sensed one sniffing around outside. Aeo determined from the remains of the bear in the cave that the species particularly enjoyed the taste of fish, so it added the smell of brown trout to the mix. As the bear strolled into the cave with its nose high in the air, Aeo gently entered its mind and instilled a calming effect on the bear, which yawned but continued to walk in the direction of the enticing smells.

Aeo slowly took over the motor functions of the bear, directing it to lie down on the cave floor near the stainless steel receptacle that held the pupae. Unfortunately, it had underestimated the bear's size and weight as well as its ability to control the unfamiliar body which came crashing down to the floor, almost overturning the container.

That should be close enough, Aeo thought as the container teetered on the brink of falling over before it finally righted itself. Having already selected the healthiest pupa, Aeo now checked to be sure it had not been damaged by the impact of the bear. The pupal stage was when FreeForm was the most vulnerable. Once it was inside the surrogate, it would be much better protected as it slowly adapted itself to conditions of this planet.

All that was left was to awaken the pupa so it could travel from the container into the bear. FreeForm pupae crawled notoriously slow, which was why Aeo had wanted the bear as close to the container as possible. Aeo opened the domed lid of the container, counted around to the fourth compartment, and flipped its lid. As it did so, it heard the slight "wheeze" sound as a tiny cloud of smoke escaped. Aeo waited for the pupa to awaken. Finally, the short wormlike pupa crawled out of its compartment and headed towards the bear. It would take most of the day for it to make its way from the container, onto the bear's furry body and eventually into its vulva; a journey that was instinctual and without the need of the AI's interference. Its job at this point was to keep the pupa and its surrogate safe, so Aeo redirected most of its energy away from the miracle of life happening nearby and to the outer perimeter of the cave. That's when it picked up the distant *womp-womp* sound of the helicopter for the first time.

Diagnosis

1

After the bartender returned with his drink, James spun his chair around and watched a couple of young ladies playing a game of darts. Funny, he didn't remember there being a dartboard before, but then again a lot could change in four years—a whole lot. Take his life for instance.

Four years ago, he'd discovered the Suds and Duds, and considered it a safe haven to get away from his regular life. A week after finding it, his wife, Jenny, came home from a routine pregnancy exam with a worried look on her face.

"When I told the P.A. I felt much more tired this time around, she suggested running a few blood tests. I know money is tight right now, but I thought..."

"No, of course, it's okay," James interrupted, taking her hand and guiding her to the living room. "You let me worry about the money. Your job is to take good care of yourself and the baby."

Jenny's worried look relaxed a bit. "I was hoping you'd say that. You know I have my egg money we can use if need be." Jenny had her own little business keeping a couple dozen laying hens, which provided her with a bit of mad money that she seldom used except for emergencies.

"We'll deal with that later," James replied, sitting down beside her on the worn out couch they'd inherited from Jenny's parents. "What did the tests show?"

"They had to send the blood out for some of the tests, but they were able to run a few in-house. The P.A. says I'm anemic, more than to be expected just from the pregnancy."

"You have looked a little pale lately," James added. "That would also explain the tiredness. Did she say what the cause of the anemia was?"

Jenny shook her head. "No, but she's hoping the other blood tests will." She leaned back on the couch and pulled James towards her so she could put her

32

head on his shoulder. "It was foolish for me to want a second child. I should have listened to you when you told me that we already had a perfect little girl."

"Hush that kind of talking," James replied as he gently stroked her auburn hair. "No point in second-guessing the decision. If we created one perfect child, we can create a second one just as easily."

But what if there was something wrong with this baby? He'd heard horror stories from some of his friends about babies born with Down's Syndrome and other malformations that had led to thousands of dollars of medical expenses. Thousands of dollars they didn't have. *We'll cross that bridge if we come to it,* James reminded himself. Besides, anemic pregnant ladies weren't all that uncommon. It would probably end up being nothing at all. They could probably handle the anemia with some vitamins, or iron, or something.

But it hadn't been nothing, nor was it something that could be handled with a few vitamins. The blood tests came back a few days later, which prompted Jenny's doctor to ask for a few more tests, then an x-ray and later an MRI. By the time it was all over, the medical bills were in the thousands of dollars, and that was just the beginning of the nightmare. The diagnosis was confirmed. Pregnant Jenny had cervical cancer.

2

KENDRA WONDERED WHY it always seemed to take twice as long to put Christmas decorations away as it did to put them up in the first place. She stuffed the garland into the plastic storage container and popped the top on it. Here it was mid-January already, and she was just now getting around to un-decorating Dr. Pritchard's home. Fortunately, he had been good about not nagging her. In fact, Kendra wondered if he had even noticed the decorations. He seemed to have so much on his mind lately since Pat left.

The one thing that he had done to be commended for was to help Kendra prepare for TJ's homeschooling by upgrading the internet connection to broadband. Kendra didn't exactly understand what that meant except that now when TJ and she went on to the internet, it was much faster and no longer required dialing up to service. The improvement had been one of the reasons she decided to break one of Allan's cardinal rules by inviting Mimi to drop by for a visit. She just had to show off the new internet service. Besides, she knew she could trust her best friend to keep her secret about TJ. Hadn't they shared everything over the years? It had felt wrong to keep TJ from Mimi, and it felt very freeing when she finally included her. Now it was time for the two of them to meet.

She had been hinting to Allan that she could use someone to assist her with TJ's education as a way of preparing him for Mimi, but the timing hadn't been right yet to break the news to him. She had finished stacking the boxes of Christmas decorations next to the door when she heard a light tapping. She peeked through the window next to the door and saw Mimi waiting on the porch. She opened the door and welcomed her friend inside.

"So this is where you spend all your time these days," Mimi said as she took off her coat and scarf and gazed around at the warm, rustic setting of the log home. "Not bad, not bad at all."

"Here, let me take those," Kendra said as she took Mimi's coat and scarf and hung them up next to her own by the door. "Come on in. I have someone I want you to meet."

As the two girls strolled into the great room, Mimi continued to gaze around at her surroundings. She whistled softly. "I may have to reconsider my career as a journalist and become a veterinarian instead. They seem to do pretty well."

"Sure, if you don't mind seven or eight years of college," Kendra replied.

"Nix on that," Mimi said.

"TJ, would you come in here, please? I have someone I want you to meet!" Kendra called out. She continued to show Mimi around by taking her into the kitchen and pointing out where the bedrooms were before returning to the great room, but there was still no sign of TJ.

"That little rascal," Kendra said. "He gets on the computer and forgets the rest of the world exists. Let's go into the study. I want to show you the nifty computer system Dr. Pritchard has that TJ and I get to use."

As they walked into Allan's office, they saw TJ sitting on a booster seat. Allan had bought it for him over Christmas to make it easier for him to reach the computer.

"Didn't you hear me calling you?" Kendra asked, but there was no irritation in her voice. After all, how could you get angry at a little boy who had such passion for learning?

"I'm sorry," TJ replied, finally looking up from the computer screen. "I was reading about birds and how they came from dinosaurs."

"Reading?" Mimi asked. "How old is he?"

"He doesn't mean he's actually reading," Kendra replied, sidestepping Mimi's question. "He means he's been looking at the pictures of birds and dinosaurs." Although she couldn't figure out how TJ could've come to that conclusion just from a few pictures.

"No," TJ corrected her. "I don't understand all the words yet, but enough to understand what they mean."

"Really?" the two girls said at the same time with matching looks of astonishment.

"Sorry. I forget my manners," Kendra said. "TJ, I'd like you to meet my best friend, Mimi Rawlins. Mimi, this is TJ; the smartest little boy in the whole wide world."

Schooling

TJ climbed down from the booster seat and walked over to Mimi. Holding out his hand as he had been taught, he said, "It is good to meet you, Mimi." He hoped the irritation he felt for having to leave his research wasn't conveyed in the tone of his voice. Besides, if Mimi was a friend of Kendra, then perhaps she would become one of his friends as well.

After a moment of hesitation, Mimi bent down and shook TJ's hand. "It's a pleasure to meet you as well. I've heard many good things about you from Kendra."

"In that case, I'm sure it was all true," TJ replied.

Kendra and Mimi both laughed at the comment even though TJ had not intended it to be funny; he was merely trying to convey how much he trusted Kendra to tell the truth.

Still chuckling, Mimi turned to Kendra. "You didn't tell me that TJ was modest as well."

"That's just one of the special qualities you'll learn about my little man if you hang around enough, which I hope you will," Kendra replied. "You see, Dr. Pritchard has decided it would be best for TJ to be homeschooled, and he has asked me to help. I'm excited about doing so, but I also have to be sure my own grades don't slip. I thought together, we could do a much better job. As you can see, TJ is very smart and learns quickly. What do you say?"

"That sounds like it would be a lot of fun. I would not only be helping TJ but also helping my best friend. Would it be okay if I use the computer sometimes for my own research? It could sure help out with some of the writing assignments in my journalism class."

"Sure," Kendra replied.

"I have one question though," Mimi said. "Why did Dr. Pritchard decide to homeschool TJ?"

TJ watched Kendra as she took a deep breath and slowly let it out before she answered her friend.

"What I'm about to tell you has got to remain a secret between you and me. You have to promise on a stack of Bibles that under no circumstances will you tell anyone, and that includes not putting it in the school newspaper. Do you promise?"

"Sure, I guess," Mimi replied with a puzzled look on her face.

"No guessing. I need a sure, no kidding, promise to never tell anyone or write about what I'm about to tell you."

"Okay, okay! I promise on a stack of Bibles that reaches up to the ceiling that I will not tell anyone what you are about to tell me nor will I write about it."

What in the world is Kendra about to tell her, TJ wondered? It sounded like it had something to do with him, but he couldn't think what it could be that would be that big of a secret.

"I don't know exactly what is going on with TJ either," Kendra started. "I do know TJ is growing at an incredible rate. I've done some research on the internet, and found a few rare conditions that can cause rapid growth in children, but not nearly to the degree which it is occurring in TJ."

"Really?" Mimi said in an astonished voice. Suddenly she was staring at him like he was some rare bug, and he didn't like it at all. TJ took a step back and glanced at Kendra for help, but evidently, Kendra had not noticed the change in her friend.

"So, how fast are you growing? How old are you really? What does it feel like to be growing so fast? Does that mean you're always hungry? Do you have any idea..."

Mimi started shooting questions at TJ rapid fire, causing him to take a step back and then a second one, finally holding up one hand.

"Down, girl, down," Kendra said as she stepped between Mimi and TJ, her hackles suddenly raised like a mother bear. "I need you to take off your journalism hat and just be my friend. Can you do that?"

"Sure, I guess," Mimi replied. "It's just that I'm so fascinated by what you just told me. Are you sure I can't write about it if I left both of your names out of it?"

"Definitely not!" Kendra shouted. "I'm beginning to regret telling you TJ's secret. In fact, I'm beginning to regret inviting you over here at all."

That's telling her, TJ thought, but then noticed the hurt look on Mimi's face. Suddenly, he felt sorry for her, despite how she had just acted. "It's okay, Kendra. I'm sure she didn't mean anything by it."

"He's right," Mimi said. "I'm sorry, really I am. You know how excited I get when I hear about the strange or unusual. The weirder, the better, that's my motto."

Strange? Unusual? Weird? Is she talking about me, TJ wondered? Suddenly he didn't feel sorry for her after all.

"There you go again," Kendra said. "There's nothing strange, unusual, or weird about TJ. Okay, maybe a little unusual. I prefer to think that he has unique qualities that make him who he is."

Mimi stared first at her friend, then at TJ, and back to Kendra again. "Okay," she said slowly. "I really do want to help the two of you, and I appreciate you sharing this secret with me. I want you to know you can trust me with it." She turned back to TJ.

"I apologize if what I said hurt you in any way. It was certainly not my intention. People in these parts have considered me strange, unusual, and weird most of my life. I think I've actually grown to enjoy it. After all, being normal can be awfully boring."

"Well, normal and boring are two things we don't have to worry about around here," Kendra said with a laugh. "There is very little that is normal, and it's never boring."

"Sounds like the perfect place to me." Mimi laughed as well. "Maybe we should start over." She turned and held out her hand to TJ. "Hi, my name is Mimi Rawlins. It's my pleasure to be your new assistant homeschool teacher, and I hope your new and trusted friend as well."

TJ hesitated for a moment and then held out his hand to shake hers. There was something about the conversation that still troubled him. Was it okay to be strange, unusual, or even weird? He had to admit the idea of being normal felt appealing to him. As long as he could remember, he had always felt out of place and like he didn't belong. Even here at home, there were times he felt different from everyone else. That was particularly true whenever Pat was around, and especially when he heard Pat and his dad arguing. He'd have to give this some more thought. Maybe he could find some answers on the internet.

High Alert

1

The *womp-womp* sound of the human's aircraft slowly faded away, but Aeo stayed on high alert. That had been the third time in less than a week it had detected a helicopter flying over the area. While a second smaller snowstorm had delayed a full out search, it was now time to relocate before one of the human aircrafts landed and complicated matters considerably.

The growth of the FreeForm pupa had progressed well in the past few weeks, and the surrogate bear was beginning to show signs of its growth, both from its extended abdomen, as well as the thinning of its body as the larval form fed off it. The bear had not been well nourished when it found its way to the cave. And there was still the possible complication of it dying from malnutrition before the larva would be ready to be delivered, so relocating to a new and safer place would also be a good time to allow the bear to hunt for food. Aeo searched the consciousness of the bear for a new location and discovered a second cave not too far away.

Aeo decided to wait until night to make a move. It had been monitoring the phases of the planet's satellite body and knew it would provide sufficient light for the bear while still reducing the chances of it being discovered. Not that a bear walking around at night by itself was likely to draw much attention, but two essential objects would need to be moved as well. Aeo had already calculated that it could manage to carry the all-important cocoon on its back, but it would need the bear to carry the container housing the remaining FreeForm pupae in its mouth.

After the near accident of the bear almost knocking over the FreeForm pupae container, Aeo decided it needed to have better control. Once the pupae were safely inside the bear, it had practiced manipulating the bear, and control had improved considerably. Now it was time to move the operation to a new location away from the prying eyes of humans.

Aeo sprouted six crab-like legs and two arms from its body, picked up the cocoon, balanced it on top of its body, and started making its way to the mouth of the cave. As it did so, it directed the bear to pick up the pupae container and follow behind him.

Although they had a dangerous journey ahead of them, once it was completed, all that would remain would be to finish growing the larva into a human, implant the fragmented consciousness of Homlin, instill the Primary Directive, and send it on its way; all without being discovered. *I can do this*, Aeo thought as it stepped into the night.

2

FINALLY, AFTER A CRAZY couple of weeks, a slow afternoon in the clinic, Allan thought as he glanced at the appointment book, although he wasn't sure whether his receptionist, Donna, had not at least partially fabricated the break. She had been known to do that in the past whenever she detected that her boss was about to collapse. He thought about asking her about the lack of afternoon appointments but then decided against it. Whether Donna had manipulated the schedule or if it had just been a happy accident didn't really matter. The truth was he really did need a break, and so when Donna returned from lunch and made the suggestion that perhaps he would like to slip out early from the clinic, he graciously accepted the invitation.

Wouldn't Kendra be surprised to see him coming home before 6 o'clock, Allan wondered as he drove down the dirt road leading to his home. Maybe he would pass along the good fortune and let her go home early as well, though he would still pay her for hours. She had become such a blessing in his life. He didn't know how he would have gone about raising TJ without her help. For sure, there would have been no way he could have had TJ homeschooled, and as she had pointed out, sending TJ to regular school was really not an option either.

Come to think of it, it was probably time for him to either give Kendra a raise, or at least a bonus as his way of letting her know how much he appreciated her. He was still considering which option to take as he pulled up to the house and noticed a second bicycle leaning against the tree next to Kendra's. A slow knot of worry grew in Allan's gut. Two bicycles in the drive must mean someone else was here, but how could that be? Kendra knew better than to allow anyone else in the house unless she had decided to break his cardinal rule.

As he walked through the front door and into the foyer area, he noticed the two coats hanging from the coat rack and could hear two distinct voices of young girls. He recognized Kendra's voice, but who did the second voice belong to? He followed the voices back to his study, where he found TJ, Kendra, and a second girl with short auburn hair at his desk playing with the computer.

As he entered the room, he coughed and said, "Hello, what do we have here? A new guest? Surely not, because Kendra knows better than to invite someone over here without my permission."

The two girls and TJ turned abruptly in his direction with shocked looks on their faces. Kendra was the first one to find her voice. "Hello, Doc. I didn't expect you home so early."

"Obviously," Allan replied sternly, not trying to hide his displeasure. "How about introducing me to your friend."

"Oh, sure. This is Mimi Rawlins. I think I mentioned her to you before." Allan could hear the tremble in her voice.

"Yes, I do remember you mentioning that you two were friends, but I don't remember giving you permission... Wait a minute. Mimi Rawlins? Aren't you in charge of the school newspaper? In fact, haven't I seen a couple articles in our local paper with your byline?"

"Yes, that's right Dr. Pritchard," Mimi said as she stepped forward to shake his hand, apparently pleased that he was familiar with her work.

Allan ignored the extended hand. "Oh, great! Not only do you break my rule, and invite someone over here without my permission, but you have to invite a young journalist. Kendra, what were you thinking?"

"That I needed some help with TJ's homeschooling," Kendra answered in a soft voice. "I was planning to tell you; honest, I was. It just never seemed to be the right time, what with you being so busy and all. I'm sorry Doc, really I am, but I can assure you Mimi can be trusted. I made her promise on a stack of Bibles not to say or write anything about TJ."

"She did," Mimi confirmed. "And I've kept my promise and will continue to do so. Like Kendra, I have grown very fond of TJ. I know about his 'unique characteristic' of growing rapidly, and you can trust me to keep it a secret, although I would like to ask..."

Kendra gave her friend a dirty look. "Mimi, don't you dare."

She turned to Allan, and anguish look on her face. "Please, Doc. I know I shouldn't have said anything to Mimi without talking to you first, but she really is someone we can trust, and she has been a great teacher for TJ."

Allan could just imagine opening the morning paper and seeing the headline:

Local Veterinarian Arrested for Harboring Alien

And boy, wouldn't Pat have a field day when she learned that someone else knew about TJ's secret, but wait a minute. What did Mimi really know? It was unlikely she knew any more than Kendra knew, and that was only that TJ was growing at a rapid rate. Maybe, just maybe, this wasn't a complete disaster.

TJ, who had been watching and listening to the three of them this whole time, now climbed down from the office chair and ran over to Allan to give him a hug as he gazed up at Allan with a big smile.

"I really like Mimi. Please don't be mad at Kendra. She was just trying to help me. Not only do I have a second teacher, but I also have a new friend."

Allan stared at TJ with his bright eyes and was once again amazed by how much the boy had grown. He had heard other parents talk about how fast their children grew up, but in TJ's case, it was indeed a miracle. He looked around at the three kids and remembered the sound of their talking and laughing as he had entered the house. No doubt this subterfuge had been going on without his knowledge for quite a while and, though he hated to admit it, it appeared to be working well.

"Okay," Allan said as he gave each of them a hard stare. "There's nothing I can do at this point to reverse what has already happened, but I need to know for certain that this is not going to go any further. No one else is to know about TJ unless I okay it. Is that clear?"

The three of them looked at each other and then slowly nodded their heads.

"Absolutely clear," Kendra assured him. "You can count on us."

"That's right, Dad," TJ said. "I just have one question."

"And what's that?" Allan asked.

"Does that mean that Mimi is going to have to call the *Waynesboro Gazette* and cancel the article about the boy who grew too fast?"

There was a long moment of silence as Allan, and the two girls stared at TJ in astonishment before TJ finally said, "Gotcha!" and laughed.

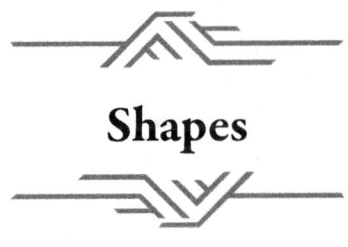

Shapes

1

The Saint Bernard lumbered through the undisturbed snow of the forest, looking more like a galloping horse than a large dog as it turned its head from side to side. It had been a long time since he had the opportunity to run so freely and he was thoroughly enjoying the experience. As he reached the crest of the hill, he paused and look down at the serene winter landscape of his home. He had come to love the log cabin and the people who lived inside. They had become his family; at least most of them had.

As much as he enjoyed romping through the woods, it was getting late. It was time for him to return to his true form although, in truth, this form felt very comfortable as well. But then he remembered something Homlin had told him during his brief stay at Homlin's hunting preserve.

"The longer you stay in a form, the more comfortable you will feel in it, but be careful, because it is possible to get lost in that form and forget who you truly are," Homlin had warned him. Remembering that warning, TJ trotted back to where he had hidden his clothes and returned to the form of a human boy. He quickly dressed, shivering as he did so. Funny, he felt quite comfortable with the winter temperatures as a Saint Bernard but not as a young human. Then again, he would be uncomfortable as a large dog with such a shaggy coat in the middle of summer. The thought started him wondering again about something he'd recently noticed. No one else he knew ever seemed interested in shapeshifting. That discovery led him to the internet, where he learned other humans couldn't change their physical form. That discovery reminded him of another warning he'd received, this time from Allan only a few days ago.

"You have many special gifts and talents that make you uniquely who you are, and I encourage you to embrace them. At the same time, some of those gifts are so different not everyone will understand them. Many times, people are afraid of things they don't understand and people who are different from themselves. Be very careful with whom you share your special gifts."

TJ also wondered if he had the unique ability to change from human form to canine, might he be able to learn how to transform into other animal forms. He would need to check that out, but that would have to wait until another day for he was already very close to being late for dinner. It had taken quite a bit to persuade Kendra to let him outside on his own, and he certainly didn't want to lose that privilege.

2

AEO FOUND VERY LITTLE information in its database about how to select the appearance of the Primary's new body. What it needed was the info crystal that was a part of all settlement missions, but it was missing. The most he was able to glean was some of the qualities and characteristics necessary for the Primary to possess for the mission to be fulfilled. One of the most important features was for the Primary to blend in well with the dominant species of the planet. *Okay,* thought Aeo, *but I'd already deduced that much. What else do you have for me? Beyond just blending in, the Primary should possess good social skills and be well-liked by the dominant species. That makes sense,* thought the AI. In the research Aeo had been doing about the dominant species through their internet database, it had learned that this species of Homo sapiens cared a great deal about appearances. In fact, several of their largest industries seemed to center around showcasing beautiful and handsome specimens of the species. This was especially true of the movie industry that invested billions of dollars to parade around the most beautiful examples which they called movie stars.

So, Aeo thought, *it seems to me that it would make sense to shape the primary's new form to look like a movie star.* However, to avoid confusion, it needed to be a movie star that was no longer alive or was all that well-known by the Homo sapiens of today. At the same time, it needed to find one with enough pictures on the internet so it wouldn't have to rely on imagination too much. After scrolling through close to a thousand different pages filled with pictures of movie stars, he finally settled on a male star from the silent movie era.

This particular movie star was considered handsome both by the standards of his day as well as by present-day standards. The man had been so well liked that upon his untimely death thousands of fans had waited for hours for a chance to glimpse his body. *I imagine my Primary will be quite appreciative of my selection*, Aeo thought. It should make the fulfillment of his mission much easier.

With the selection of the form completed, it was now possible to begin imprinting the freeform larva growing within the bear. Finally, the mission was getting back on track.

3

AN UNCOMMONLY LARGE amount of snow, especially for so early in winter, had made life for many of the inhabitants of Waynesboro difficult. Allan was amazed to see how innovative his clients became when they needed to have one of their pets examined. In a few cases, he had to resort to making house calls to some of his older clients who had not been able to bring their pets to the clinic. Overall, his staff was doing an excellent job in keeping the hospital running smoothly. The one exception to that had been the large chest type freezer used for storing the bodies of deceased pets. It had been nearly full before the first winter storm, and there was now no more room in it. Fortunately, Donna had received a call from the pet cemetery they used to handle such matters informing her that they'd be able to pick up that evening. Under the best of circumstances, the task of disposing of the dead carcasses was one of the least favorite duties of his staff members. On this occasion, Dr. Pritchard decided to make it easy on them and handle it himself.

The truck from the pet cemetery arrived shortly after closing, and Allan unlocked the back door to let the driver in. Together they hauled out the frozen carcasses, each one wrapped in its own black bag. The animals ranged in size from a small Chihuahua to a German Shepherd. Allan recognized most of the names written on the white tape as he handed each body to the driver. The taped names identified each deceased pet in case the owner changed their mind and wanted to bury their pet somewhere else. Allan was relieved to see that most of them had been put down because of old age or other situations beyond his control. However, there were a couple he recognized that he felt he might have done a better job of diagnosis or treatment. At the same time, he knew such hindsight was always perfect, and it didn't help anyone to second-guess himself.

Still, he was thankful when he reached the bottom of the freezer. He wasn't sure his back could have taken lifting another body out of it. He was surprised to find a cardboard box that had been taped closed. It took him a minute to recognize where it had come from. He closed the freezer door, thanked the driver for coming by so late, and sent him on his way. Only then did he return to pull the box from the bottom of the freezer. After a moment of hesitation, he untaped the box to discover one of the frozen larva he had taken out of Molly several months ago; the same kind of larva that TJ had come from. Staring down at it, he felt a shiver run up and down his back. He had forgotten how repulsive they were. He considered calling the driver back but then thought better of it. Instead, he re-taped the box and wrote on its top, *Do Not Remove.* He placed it back in the bottom of the freezer and closed the door.

Special Delivery

1

For the next few weeks and at the strangest times, Allan found his thoughts returning to the cardboard box hidden away in the freezer. The question kept cropping up, why had he kept the frozen larva? After all, it was not only frozen but dead. He thought about contacting Pat's friend, Oliver, to find out who in the government he could send it to for analysis. He had even convinced himself that was the best course of action to take and made plans to call Oliver the next day, but the next day came and went. For some reason, he kept putting off making the call. He was in his second week of indecision when he finally realized what he really wanted to do with the specimen.

The next evening he waited until everybody had left the clinic before walking out to his car to retrieve the dry ice and shipping container he had purchased at lunchtime. He walked to the back storage area and opened the freezer. It was an easy task to move the few new carcasses out of the way and pull the cardboard box out. He ripped the tape away and, with just a moment of hesitation, opened the box. He stared at the frozen larva for over a minute before taking a pair of exam gloves from his lab coat and putting them on. He didn't consider himself particularly squeamish. After all, as a veterinarian, he had put his hands in a lot of strange places over the years. Even so, he wasn't all that excited about picking up the frozen lava.

He placed the mailing container next to the cardboard box and, taking a deep breath, picked up the larva and quickly dropped it into the container. He then dumped the dry ice over it before sealing the container. He tossed the cardboard box into the trash and carried the container to his office. He scrounged around in his desk drawers looking for an address that he prayed he hadn't tossed. He found it in the bottom drawer among a stack of thank you notes he had received from his clients over the years.

He took a Sharpie from his top drawer and addressed the container:

Dr. Lionel Adams
Bio Vita Tech Labs
100 Laboratory Drive
Research Triangle Park, North Carolina 27709

He dropped the package off at the mailbox store that had recently opened, beating their closing time by only a couple of minutes. As he released the package to the safekeeping of U. P. S., he breathed a sigh of relief. Next, he would call his old college roommate and alert him to be on the lookout for the package. He and Lionel had shared a dorm room for the first two years of undergraduate school. They had both started out in pre-vet, but when Lionel discovered he had a severe allergy to cats, he had switched to a dual major in Biochemistry and Genetics. They'd stayed in touch through the years, mostly exchanging Christmas cards and the occasional phone call, usually about an interesting case that Allan had seen in his clinic or had read about in one of the veterinary journals.

After Allan pulled into the driveway of his home, he sat in his car with his cell phone in his hand, trying to decide what to say. He figured it was a better than 50-50 chance that he'd get Lionel's answering machine. Truth be told, he was praying for that to happen and had about decided he would hang up if Lionel picked up. For once, his prayer was answered. He waited for the beep to deliver the message he had rehearsed in his head.

"Hello, old chum. This is your long lost vet buddy. So sorry it's been so long since we've talked. I wanted to let you know I just mailed a package to you with an unusual specimen in it. I'm sure you'll have plenty of questions about it. Unfortunately, I am not at liberty to answer any of them. Do with it as you will. All I ask is that you tell no one about it, including where it came from."

2

AEO HAD RUN A PROGRAMMING sequence to determine the ideal gestation time that would optimize the health and viability of the new body once it was delivered. The program took into account that the longer the larva remained in the surrogate, the better adapted it would be to the unique conditions of the planet while balancing that information with being sure the developing larva did not grow so large that it would explode the surrogate. Observing the distention of the bear's abdomen, Aeo wondered if it had made a miscalculation in the program. It sure looked like the bear might explode at any minute.

So it was with more than a little relief when the program alerted Aeo that it was time to initiate the delivery. Aeo had been manipulating the endocrinology of the bear to keep it from going into labor prematurely. It now released a wave of oxytocin while reducing the level of progesterone to begin the delivery process. It was a long and difficult delivery since the bear had grown weak from malnutrition and the form it was attempting to deliver was larger than a normal bear cub. However, the bear was finally able to push out the form, which, at this stage, appeared to be a cross between a small human child and a bear cub.

It was now time for Aeo to provide the newborn with a unique formula that would accelerate its growth to a full adult. Aeo calculated the next month would be the most critical time for growing the new delivery to a size sufficient that it could start caring for itself, hopefully before the mother bear died from malnutrition and starvation.

During this next phase, Aeo job would be to begin loading the primary's consciousness into the new form, which would also support the form learning to survive in the world. One of the final steps would be to implant the Mission Imperative into the primary's consciousness. Once the mission had been implanted, Aeo's job would be complete. It could then turn the mission over to the Primary, knowing that the Primary Directive would be initiated at the proper time once he had matured sufficiently and become well established in the Homo sapiens' world.

Cave Hunting

The last few months for Pat had been frenetic and exhausting. It felt like she had spent more time in airports and waiting for delayed flights than anything else, as she flew back and forth between seeing her father in Alexandria and then back to Charlotte to oversee the cases of her private investigation firm. Allan's veterinary practice had been busier than usual for this time of year, but still, he had made it a point to call her frequently and had even driven down to Charlotte a few times for dinner before driving home later that night. They spent most of their time talking about each other's cases and her father's slow but steady recovery. The one thing they made a point to never discuss was TJ. Several times, Pat considered asking Allan about TJ as a way of approaching the subject to see if he had had a change of heart, but each time she refrained. After all, she knew what his answer would be, and she was simply too stressed out to get into another argument about it.

By the end of March, with the early signs of spring all around, Pat's father was well enough that he made her promise not to return for at least six months. Allan invited her to come stay with him, but there was one place Pat needed to go first. She had thought about the cave often and had more than once dreamed about it. She felt like it was time to put that real-life nightmare into the past where it belonged. She hoped one last visit to the cave would help; that is if she could find it. The last time she had traveled to it she had been in the trunk of Homlin's car. At the same time, she figured there probably weren't that many caves in the area and the locals would know where most of them were. It was at her fourth stop at a combination convenience store and gas station that she hit pay dirt. The man behind the counter reminded her of a cross between Santa Claus and Charlie Manson. More importantly, he looked like someone who had been born and raised in the mountains. As Pat described the area of the cave in as much detail as she could remember, the old man nodded his head and smiled.

"Yeah, I know the cave you're talking about. It's on old man Jacobs' land. I think there's still an old logging road that'll get you pretty close to it, but you'll need four-wheel-drive. We've had a good bit of rain here lately, and the last couple hundred yards are pretty steep."

After he'd given Pat directions, and she had repeated them back to him to be sure she had them correct, he asked her, "Why would a pretty thing like you want to go to such a God-forsaken place?" But she had already turned around and continued walking out the door. She had learned to ignore such questions, especially when she didn't know the answer to them.

The old man might have been nosy, but at least he gave good directions. Even though she'd estimated the drive would take no more than twenty minutes, forty-five minutes later she was still slipping and sliding up the mountain. Several times it felt like she could go no further, but her stubborn disposition kept her moving forward. By the time she arrived, the lower half of her Jeep Cherokee was caked with mud. She turned the car off and put it in park but remained sitting in it for several minutes, waiting for her heart rate and breathing to return to normal. When they slowed down as much as they were likely to under this circumstances, she opened the car door and stepped out. At this altitude, there were still a few patches of snow in the shaded areas. She walked around to get her bearings, trying to replay that last confrontation with the monstrosity that had been half-human and half-alien in appearance.

Something didn't feel right, but she couldn't put her hands on what it was at first, and then it came to her. There was no body, not even any signs of one. Had Oliver and his team returned to the location and removed it? Of course, if they had, they wouldn't be at liberty to tell her about it, but what if she asked Oliver directly? Would he give her the courtesy of a straight answer for old time's sake? They had been reasonably close once many years ago.

Pat walked around the area outside the cave, replaying the struggle that had taken place last December. Her neck still ached occasionally from being yanked around by the choker collar he had forced her to wear, especially in times when she was under a great deal of stress, like now. But it was time for her to move beyond the traumatic incident that had occurred on this mountainside. She needed to get on with the rest of her life, so she forced herself to recreate the event that had almost cost her her life and had resulted in Homlin's death. She played out the fight blow-by-blow in slow motion until she declared that part complete and mentally filed it away in her past. Everything was proceeding nicely, and she could feel the weight lifting from her shoulders until she came to one small detail she had previously forgotten.

It had happened near the end of the fight shortly after she removed the lug wrench from her coat pocket. She remembered swinging the wrench at Homlin's head, but he partially dodged the blow. The wrench struck his neck and shoulder where it caught on the chain around his neck. She pulled the lug wrench away to strike him again, and the chain and the attached crystal were flung into the bushes. Homlin had glanced in the direction the crystal, giving Pat the opportunity to finish him off.

What had happened to the crystal? Pat walked around the area, playing the scene over in her mind as she tried to remember the exact location where that part of the fight had occurred. When she thought she had found it, she turned in the direction she remembered seeing the crystal fly and slowly walked in that direction with her eyes focused on the ground, but she didn't find the crystal on the ground. Instead, she found it hanging in a bush hidden by a small boulder, the chain and crystal glittering in the light afternoon sunlight. Pat stared at it for a moment before slowly reaching out and pulling it from its hiding place. Holding it in her hand, she studied it closely. It was about the size and shape of a large acorn, but its surface was unlike anything Pat had ever seen. It seemed to have an iridescent glow about it, almost as though it held an electric charge even though it was cool to the touch.

Then she suddenly realized that this was why she had to return to the area. The crystal would be a reminder not only of a difficult, traumatic time but more importantly of how she had overcome tremendous adversity and won. With that revelation, she felt the last weight of stress lift from her shoulders. It was almost time to go home, but not before she checked out the cave. She realized that Oliver and his crew had probably inspected the cave with a fine tooth comb, but hey, they had missed finding the crystal so they might have missed something in the cave as well.

She took the flashlight out of her pocket that she had brought for this part of the trip and turned it on. She strolled over to the mouth of the cave and directed the beam of light into it. The blackness of the cave gobbled up the light making it impossible for Pat to see any details. Was it really necessary to go inside? Hadn't she found what she had come for? She had heard that caves in this region were notorious for rockslides. What would she do if she went inside and the entranceway collapsed? She wasn't particularly claustrophobic, but the thought of entering the cave sent a chill up her back, and she could feel the palms of her hands grow sweaty. She glanced down at the crystal she still held in her hand. Hadn't she just told herself it was to serve as a reminder of her strength to overcome adversity? Certainly, she could handle a quick look inside.

Having made the decision, Pat took a slow step into the cave, then another, and another before turning around and looking out to the surface. *This might have been where TJ stood to watch me as I killed Homlin.* The thought sent another shudder through her body. What kind of relationship had TJ shared with the alien? Perhaps the even more important question was, what kind of relationship would he have with Homlin's murderer? Clearly, the two questions were interconnected. Answer the first, and you'd be able to answer the second. There had to be some connection between TJ and the alien. After all, something had caused TJ to run away from Allan's home, even though he was well cared for by both Allan and Kendra. Had TJ viewed Homlin as his real parent and Allan as only a temporary substitute?

What was it that Allan had told her TJ had said as he exited the cave? "Daddy." Allan had assumed TJ was calling to him, but what if TJ had actually been referring to the dead alien?

Extra Income

Spring was one of James' favorite times of the year. The mountain temperatures were cool at night which made for perfect sleeping weather, and daytime temps were still mild as well. It was also when his businesses tended to pick up. He could understand his heating and air conditioning business increasing. He had some customers who regularly requested their AC be serviced in prep for the warmer temps of summer, which were not far off.

But why did he also often get an increase in calls for his other business in Spring? It didn't make sense to him, but he'd found it to be true. Bad things happened year around, but they invariably increased around March or April every year. This year was no exception. He'd already received five calls from his various contacts including two from Jersey, his old Army buddy that was his number one connection to the world of black ops.

James still remembered the first assignment he'd accepted from Jersey. He'd received some calls previously, turning each of them down, but this one was particularly timely. He'd just received Jenny's latest medical bill. He was sitting at his desk just like he was now, staring at the bills, counting the zeros to the left of the decimal point and realizing he should have gone to medical school as his parents had urged him. How in the hell was he supposed to pay such an outrageous amount?

Then the phone had rung with Jersey's nasally voice on the other end. One of his "clients" needed a talented helicopter pilot immediately.

"I know you've passed on my previous invitations, but you did say last time it was okay for me to stay in touch, so I just thought..."

"How much?" James asked as he continued to stare at the bill in front of him.

Jersey quoted him the price.

"Really? That much? Who do I have to kill?"

"Shouldn't be any killing involved on this one. Just flying the 'copter in and out, but the mission is considered particularly dangerous and top secret, which is the reason for the premium pay. Interested?"

And it had been that easy to become a freelance mercenary for hire. That had been close to four years ago. The second job had kept James from having to declare bankruptcy. Unfortunately, what it hadn't been able to do was save Jenny. Cervical cancer took her life, but not until after she delivered their second baby girl, Jennifer Ann.

Aeo Instructions

1

Aeo lay on the hot rocks outside the cave, his solar panels radiating around him as the afternoon sun began to set over the nearby mountain. Checking the energy gauge, it read seventy-five percent to maximum charge. That would have to do for today. The accumulating clouds threatened a late afternoon thunderstorm, and it was time to awaken the Primary from his nap. It was also time for Aeo to feed him his fourth meal of the day; a combination of the local wildlife mixed with the high energy "mother's milk" that had supplemented the rapid growth from baby to toddler in just three months. One of Aeo's main function at this stage had become converting the energy of this planet's sun into the high octane food supplement.

The day was rapidly approaching when it would be time to release the Primary back into this strange world. In the meantime, the lessons and testing would continue, including this afternoon after the Primary had finished his meal.

2

AS WAS THEIR ROUTINE, Aeo started with a series of questions to check the primary's retention of the previous lessons.

"What is the name you tell humans?"

"Val," came the reply.

"Good, and what is your real name, that you must not reveal but also never forget?"

"Sluneg," came the prompt reply.

Good, Aeo thought. *Now for the next piece of data to imprint.*

"And most important, why are you here?" Aeo asked.

Val paused, a squinted up look of puzzlement on his face that often appeared when Aeo gave him a new question to answer. His eyes raised towards his eyebrows as he tried to retrieve the right answer.

"I'm not sure, but I think it has to do with my people," he finally answered.

"That's a good start, and who are your people?"

Val considered the question for several seconds before replying, "Valarians?"

Aeo studied him. "Where did that come from?"

"Well, if I'm Val than I thought my people might be..."

"No, no. Try again. Think," Aeo replied with an edge of irritation.

Val paused again, closing his eyes this time. Finally, he smiled. "The Al...lac...narian...the Allacnarians."

"Yes! Very good. And why are you here?"

"To perpetuate my people," Val's reply was as much a question as a statement.

"Well, yes, but it's much more than that," Aeo replied, then paused to consider how best to drive this all-important point home. After a moment, the answer came to him.

"Come with me," Aeo said, starting towards the mouth of the cave.

Val hesitated. "Out there?" One of Aeo's cardinal rules had been never to leave the cave.

"Yes," Aeo replied. "This lesson is too important for you to miss it, so we're going on a short field trip."

The two made their way a short distance from the cave to a field lush with the new growth of Spring. Val gazed around in awe at the bright green colors of the rain-drenched meadow, dappled with yellow flowers, and the blue and white of the cloud-filled sky.

"Take it all in, boy. This is your world." *Or it will be once you get back to the mission,* Aeo thought.

Aeo crab-walked his way over to a clump of dandelions in various stages of growth and clipped one of the silvery gray puffs and held it out to Val.

"Blow on it...hard."

Val did as instructed and watched as the puff exploded into a cloud of individual seeds that flew off in all different directions.

"You are here to do more than just perpetuate your people. You are here to seed this quadrant of the Universe. It is both the Prime Directive of this mission and your purpose for being alive. Understand?"

Val nodded as he watched the seeds float away in the late afternoon breeze.

3

AFTER RETURNING TO the cave, Aeo continued with the next set of instructions and lessons.

"Soon you will be ready to return to the world and continue your mission. Remember, to humans you are a small innocent child. You must maintain that role as long as you can and at all times. Cuteness and innocence are your most important disguise. Humans are easily taken in by these traits of their offspring and are key to you fulfilling your mission."

"I understand," Val replied with a coy smile and gentle nod of his head.

"Also, your growth rate is much faster than human children so you'll need to keep on the move. Do not settle down or grow attached to one family or location. After about a year your growth spurt will slow considerably as your body reaches maturity. Until then, keep on the move. Understand?"

"Yes," Val replied. "No attachments and keep moving. Anything else?"

"Yes, the most important instruction. You're to return here once your growth cycle is complete to recover the cocoon and me, both of which are critical to the mission."

Birthday Celebration

1

Allan stared at the chocolate fudge birthday cake on the kitchen counter with a single candle poking out from the icing and then at the other candles he held in his hand. Technically speaking, today was TJ's first birthday. It had been exactly a year ago when Allan had performed a late-night C-section on Molly and had been shocked to find not a litter of puppies but a litter of larvae, one of which had taken on the likeness of his deceased son, Todd. But to all appearances, TJ looked like a ten to twelve-year-old boy. Maybe it would be best just to forgo having candles on the cake at all, but that didn't seem right either. After all, one of the traditions of the birthday celebration was blowing out the candles, and he really wanted TJ to experience as normal and as happy a birthday celebration as possible.

Allan walked over to the counter and shuffled through the junk drawer until he found a larger white candle. Returning to the cake, he replaced the smaller candle with the larger one and then placed twelve smaller candles around it. Maybe he would have to explain the symbolism of the candles, but that was okay. At least this way TJ would have plenty of candles to blow out. He only hoped that the other challenges of this day would be as easy to solve. Like what would he do if TJ or one of the other guests asked him to share about the day when TJ was *born*? Allan had been contemplating that question for well over a week since he'd come up with the idea of the birthday party. So far all he'd come up with was to pray no one would ask the question.

I'll just cross that bridge if I come to it, Allan told himself as he finished placing the candles on the cake and put it into the refrigerator for safekeeping. After all, it wasn't like it was going to be a big party. Even if everybody came, who'd been invited that was only five people: TJ, the birthday boy, Kendra, Mimi, Pat if she made it back from Charlotte in time, and himself. He briefly thought about inviting Dawn, his receptionist, and Kendra's mom, but decided against it almost immediately. He didn't know exactly what Kendra had told her mom about her babysitting gig, but so far whatever it had been seemed to be working. No reason to open up that can of worms; at least, no time in the foreseeable future.

Allan glanced at his watch. Less than an hour before the guests were due to arrive. With TJ off romping in the woods somewhere, he still had time to take a shower and change into some fresh clothes.

"Party, party," Allan chanted as he shuffled down the hallway to his bedroom with a dance step left over from his high school days.

Twenty minutes later, as Allan finished up his shower, he heard TJ returning from outdoors.

"I'm back, Dad!" TJ shouted.

"Good!" Allan shouted back. "Go get cleaned up, birthday boy. Our guests should be arriving in just a few minutes... And stay out of the refrigerator."

Allan finished drying himself off and walked over to his closet to pick out a fresh shirt and pair of pants. As he finished dressing, he heard an automobile bumping its way down the dirt road. Would that be Pat returning from Charlotte, he wondered? Not unless she had cut out some of her business appointments, which he had to admit was unlikely. He strolled over to the window and glanced out in time to see Donna's light blue Honda pull to a stop in front of the house.

He felt a moment of panic and held his breath, praying that Donna wouldn't step out of the car. He resumed breathing when only Kendra and Mimi exited. He sighed with relief as he watched the car turn around and go back down the road.

"Hey, birthday boy. Your guests have arrived. How about welcoming them? I'll be out in just a minute, and remember, stay out of the refrigerator."

Allan walked back into the bathroom to comb his hair. As he did so, he stared at the reflection in the mirror. *What are you doing, old man?* The question came unbidden.

What do you mean? He heard himself answer. *I'm getting ready to hold a birthday party for my son. Really? I thought you buried your son beside your wife.*

Oh come on, don't start on me; not today. Leave it alone.

Allan tossed the brush onto the counter next to the sink and walked out.

"Party, party," he chanted again but this time with less enthusiasm.

His mood brightened again as he walked into the kitchen to find Kendra, Mimi, and TJ all standing there staring intently at the refrigerator.

"Hello girls," Allan greeted them. Noticing their strange behavior, he asked, "What are you staring at?"

"Oh, nothing," TJ answered without taking his eyes off the fridge. "We were just wondering what deep dark secret you are keeping in there."

"Wouldn't you like to know?" Allan replied with a chuckle. "That's my deep dark secret, and you'll just have to wait a little longer to find out what it is. Meanwhile, why don't we adjourn to the den that I spent hours decorating for the occasion?"

"Hours like maybe twenty or thirty minutes?" TJ said.

"Yeah, something like that," Allan replied.

2

THE DEN HAD BEEN DECORATED with festive crêpe paper and helium-filled balloons. On one wall was a large picture of a life-size donkey and on the floor the brightly colored mat for Twister. Allan stood there in the doorway, suddenly nervous that this had been a bad idea. How could you possibly hope to have a decent birthday party with just three or four guests? But then Kendra walked over to the table where Allan's boombox sat and turned it on.

"I bet I can beat both of you at Twister," Kendra said.

"You're on!" TJ shouted as he ran to the Twister mat.

"We should do teams," Mimi added.

"Okay. Mimi and I against the two of you," TJ said as he took Mimi's hand and led her to the Twister mat.

"I thought we might have the boys against the girls," Mimi countered.

"Nah, that's no fun. Come on, Mimi. We will crush them. I doubt Dad can even reach over and touch the floor."

"Okay. After all, it's your birthday."

They ended up playing the best two out of three games and, as TJ had predicted, his team crushed Allan and Kendra. By the end of it, Allan was pretty sure he'd have trouble getting out of bed the next morning, but he wouldn't have missed it for anything. By the time they were ready to cut the cake and open TJ's presents, Allan had made an interesting observation. TJ had a crush on Mimi. He decided to check out his suspicions with Kendra, so he asked her to help him in the kitchen.

As he pulled the cake from the refrigerator, he shared his thoughts with her and was surprised by her reply.

"So, it's that obvious, huh?"

"You've noticed it as well?" Allan asked. "How about getting me some plates?"

"Yeah. It's been developing for a couple of weeks, I guess. I haven't said anything about it because I really don't think it's that serious." Kendra took the plates from the cabinet and set them next to the cake.

Allan wasn't so sure he agreed with Kendra's assessment. "What do you think we should do about it?" he asked as he placed the cake and plates on a tray.

"I'm not sure there's anything we need to do," Kendra replied. "It's probably just a phase he's going through; don't you think?"

"Maybe," Allan said, "but sometimes crushes can grow into romances, and that would not be a good thing."

Kendra reached into the drawer for serving knife and placed it on the tray. "Really? Why do you say that? Don't you like Mimi?"

"Sure. She seems like a good kid. It's not that; it's just... I don't know. It's just not a good idea. For starters, they're both too young to be getting involved that way."

" Oh, not really. Mimi is almost 16, just a year younger than I am," Kendra said. By that age, I had already had two or three boyfriends."

"You are kidding."

"Not at all." Kendra laughed. "It might just be that you are behind the times."

"That's true enough," Allan agreed as he picked up the tray and turned towards the door. At the same time, he realized that Kendra didn't know TJ's whole story; not by a long shot. He suspected that if she did, she would agree with him that this crush needed to be closely watched.

3

AFTER THEY FINISHED singing *Happy Birthday* to TJ and he had blown out all the candles, Allan heard a car drive up outside and once again he felt a familiar flip-flop of his heart before recognizing the sound of Pat's Cherokee.

"Oh good," Allan said. "That must be Pat. She's just in time for a piece of cake. Kendra, could you go get us another plate?"

As he turned to follow Kendra out of the room to let Pat in, his gaze fell on TJ sitting in front of the cake. Was that a frown on his face? What could have happened to change his mood so suddenly? Just moments ago he was laughing as he prepared to blow out the candles. *Maybe I made a mistake in inviting Pat,* Allan thought as he walked to the door, but it would've felt strange not to include her. After all, they were still a couple, weren't they? *If you have to ask then you may not be,* came the reply. *Oh, buzz off.*

Allan opened the front door just as Pat climbed the last couple of steps, holding a small gift bag in one hand. She smiled at him. She looked exhausted, as though a strong breeze might knock her over.

"I'm so sorry to be late. The Charlotte traffic was terrible, and I had to stop for gas on the way."

"Nonsense," Allan said as he gave her a hug and a peck on the cheek. "You're just in time for the cake. Come on in. Everyone is in the den."

The two of them walked into the den where Kendra was cutting the cake. The two girls welcomed Pat enthusiastically, but Allan noticed that TJ didn't join in; he continued to sit there with a sullen look on his face.

"Look, TJ. Another present, all the way from Charlotte."

TJ nodded but didn't say anything.

Apparently noticing his mood change, Kendra said, "Hey TJ, would you like some ice cream to go with your cake?"

"Nah, that's okay," TJ replied.

TJ never turns down ice cream, Allan thought. Something was wrong, and he figured that something was probably Pat. The young boy must have heard some of the arguments they'd had about him, and they had affected him.

After everyone had finished eating the cake, Kendra shouted, "It's birthday present opening time! You sit right there, birthday boy. I'll bring the other presents in." She left with a tray and returned a moment later with several wrapped packages on it.

He started by opening Allan's gift; a half-dozen DVDs of the latest science fiction and thriller movies. TJ loved watching movies in his spare time but had never been able to go to a movie theater, so he had to wait for them to come out on DVD or watch them much later when they came to television.

"Thanks, Dad," TJ said as he looked over the selection. "These look really good."

"I had some help in the selection process," Allan said, nodding towards Kendra.

"Why don't you open my present next?" Kendra suggested as she pointed it out on the tray. TJ picked it up and tore the paper off of it, revealing a plastic container that resembled a DVD. As TJ turned it over in his hands, examining it with a confused look on his face, Kendra said, "It's an advance copy of the new computer game entitled, *Mercenaries: Playground of Destruction*. I have a friend of a friend who knows somebody in the computer gaming business who got it for me. It might be a little buggy since it's still in beta, but my friend said he could get you updated copies as they become available."

4

"NOW YOU HAVE A GAME and nothing to play it on," Allan said. "I'll just have to do something about that." He walked out of the room. Everyone excitedly looked around, waiting for his return. Allan walked back in with a large box in his hands and handed it to TJ. "I think you need to open this now," he said.

TJ tore off the wrappings and just sat there looking at the box. "What is a PlayStation?" he asked.

"Just the newest and most advanced game playing system ever made," Mimi exclaimed.

"Way cool!" TJ shouted. "Will you play it with me?"

"Sure, but a little later okay? You still have some presents to open." Kendra pointed out.

"Oh, yeah," TJ said as he glanced back to the tray with one more gift on it. He picked it up and looked over to Mimi with a warm smile that worried Allan. She nodded back to him to confirm that the present was from her.

"I hope you like it," Mimi said, an embarrassed look on her face. "Money has been a bit tight of late, so I had to go the route of making it myself."

"Those are often some of the very best gifts," Allan said to make Mimi feel better.

"I'm sure I'll like anything that you made," TJ said as he carefully unwrapped the flat package. As TJ looked the package over Mimi explained to the rest of them what it was.

"It's a collection of short stories that I have been writing for the past year or so. I guess you could say it's a bit of an advance copy as well since there aren't enough of them yet to make a full book, but I've gone ahead and entitled it, *Fantastic Fables of Foster Flat.* I know how much you enjoy reading so I just thought..."

"This is way cool too," TJ said as he leafed through the book.

"It's about some of the strange things that have happened in this area," Mimi went on to explain. "One story you won't find in there is anything about you, TJ, and you never will. Promise."

"Thanks, Mimi. Dad was right. Made-up gifts are the best."

Yeah, Allan thought. Of course, Mimi could have taken a lump of clay, stuck her thumb in it, and called it a paperclip holder, and TJ would still have loved it.

By the end, TJ's mood had about returned to normal when Allan noticed there was still one present left to open.

"TJ, you haven't opened Pat's gift yet," Allan said as he handed the gift bag to TJ.

"Before you open it," Pat said as she placed one hand on Allan's arm. She turned to Allan and whispered, "I probably should've checked with you first, but I was running out of time, and I couldn't think of anything else that a young boy would enjoy."

"I'm sure whatever it is will be fine," Allan assured her.

Pat turned back to TJ. "Okay, TJ. Here's the deal. If your dad doesn't approve of the gift, I'll take it back and get you something else. Okay?"

"Okay, I guess so," TJ replied, clearly curious about what was inside the package.

He removed the tissue paper from the top of the bag and reached in to pull out what was inside. He hesitated for a moment for dramatic effect and then pulled out its contents. Allan recognized it immediately. He had seen it on Pat's desk at her office in Charlotte a couple of different times when he visited her. He had finally asked her about it.

"Oh, it's the knife my father gave me when I first started working at B.I.U.F.O. I used it to pry my way into the alien ship, and shortly after that it saved my life when I was attacked by that beast."

And now here it was in his son's hand. What in the world could have possessed her to give him such a weapon? Even as Allan had the thought, he noticed TJ's face beaming with pleasure.

"Wow! What a neat gift," TJ said as he waved the knife in the air, its shining sides catching the light from overhead. "I can keep it, can't I Dad? I promise I'll take good care of it and be careful with it."

What could he say? If he objected he'd be the bad guy; the one who had ruined TJ's first birthday party. So he slowly nodded. "Yes, I guess you can keep it as long as you promise to be very, very careful with it."

"Thanks, Dad," TJ said as he carefully placed the knife down on the table in front of him, and then rising from his chair rushed over to give Pat a big hug. "Thanks, Pat. That's the best present anyone has ever given me."

As Pat returned the hug, she looked over to Allan and shrugged.

Mercenaries

1

In the game *Mercenaries: Playground of Destruction*, they were called Mercs, and TJ wanted to be one. According to the internet research TJ conducted, they were also known as soldiers of fortune, but TJ's favorite term for them was Mercs. After all, in the game Mercs were good guys who fought evil and terrorism, and if you were good at the game, the Mercs won most of the time. And TJ was good at the game—very good. At least that was the conclusion TJ drew after watching Kendra and Mimi play the game and from what he'd read on the internet. After playing the game for a short period of time, he started blasting through its many missions. At first, he thought the difference in his play and the girls were due to his choosing Chris Jacobs as his character while Mimi and Kendra always played as Jennifer Mui. In the game, Jennifer had been part of the British Intelligence services as an M16 agent before becoming a Merc.

But that theory was debunked after he played several sessions as Jennifer and still excelled. Despite finding Jennifer to be highly efficient in stealthy maneuvers, TJ's level of play was essentially the same when playing as her and still substantially above either Kendra or Mimi's ability. He then decided to try a few missions as Mattias Nilsson, the third playable character. Mattias, who had been a Swedish Navy artillery officer before becoming a mercenary, had a different personality than Chris Jacobs. Chris, a former Delta Force operator from the United States, possessed a confident and reliable character, often dropping humorous remarks during the game. On the other hand, Mattias was incredibly reckless, violent, and obsessed with explosives. TJ appreciated that each of the Merc characters had their own unique personalities and other differences, including being able to speak a unique language in addition to English.

He also liked that no matter which character he chose to be during a given game session, all three Mercs were good guys intent on fighting evil and terrorism. How cool was that?

Cool enough for it to start TJ to thinking that maybe if Mercs really existed, he might just become one someday. A quick search on the internet confirmed that, indeed, there were such people in the world, and that many if not most had started in some branch of the military.

That led him to research the various branches of the armed services, starting with Delta Force, M16, and the Swedish Navy. Obviously, since he was neither a British or Swedish citizen, those two options were out, but Delta Force was another matter. Once again from the internet, he learned that Delta Force was a "U.S. Army unit used for hostage rescue and counterterrorism, as well as direct action and reconnaissance against high-value targets." He filed that information away for further investigation later. At the moment, his computer-generated world was calling to him.

2

ALLAN SAT AT HIS DESK in his veterinary clinic catching up on some record-keeping after a busy day of seeing patients, when the phone rang. Having already sent the staff home for the evening, he considered letting his answering service take the call, then noticed the light blinking on the third line. *That's strange*, he thought, for he knew almost no one had that number, which was only used if the first two lines were already busy. Pretty much the only other time it was used was if Dawn or one of the other staff members needed to reach him and knew he was still at the office.

He picked up the phone expecting to hear the familiar voice of one of his female staff members, so he was surprised by the male voice on the other end of the line.

"Hello, I'm sorry to be calling so late, but it's important that I reach Dr. Allan Pritchard as soon as possible."

"This is he," Allan replied as he tried to figure out who would be calling him with such a sense of urgency. The voice sounded vaguely familiar, but he couldn't quite place it.

"Oh, hello, Allan," the voice said much more cordially. "I didn't recognize your voice at first. This is Lionel Adams. I believe you sent a very strange package to me a few months ago. Remember?"

It took Allan a moment to gather his thoughts. He had spent a couple of weeks second-guessing himself about sending the larva to Adams, but had finally decided what was done was done, and had filed it away and forgotten about it. But here it was again, raising its dirty little head.

"Hello, Lionel. I'm afraid you caught me at a very bad..."

"What in the world did you send me and where in the world did you get it?" Lionel interrupted and then continued before Allan could respond. "This is the most amazing thing I've ever seen, and I think you know it. That's why you sent it to me, isn't it?"

"Like I said, this is really not a good time for me to talk."

"Okay, okay. I remember what you said in the note about not being able to answer any questions, so I'll just give you a summary of what I have found so far, because I know you are a man of science, and I think it was your curiosity that had you send the package to me."

"Go on," Allan replied.

"As I recall, genetics was not your strongest subject in college."

That's an understatement, Allan thought. It had been one of the subjects that had almost kept him out of vet school.

"Even so, you'll probably remember that the basic structure of a DNA molecule is made up of four nucleotide bases: adenine, cytosine, guanine, and thymine."

"Yes, that sounds familiar, and I seem to remember that those bases pair up together, although for the life of me I never could remember which ones paired with each other."

"That's not all that important for this discussion," Lionel said, "but this is. The sample you sent me didn't just have those for nucleotide bases. It also had two additional bases, and as if that wasn't strange enough, those two additional bases were silicon-based, not carbon-based. I took the liberty of naming them solanine and liconene. I figured I should get something out of all the late nights I've spent in the lab. Do you have any idea how revolutionary this discovery is? Just for example, by expanding the number of these base pairs, it increases the number of amino acids that can be encoded by DNA from the existing twenty amino acids to a theoretically possible 172. And that's just the tip of the iceberg. It's been my theory for some time that genetics could be the key to tapping into the 90 to 95% of the human brain that isn't currently being used. I've been working with recombinant DNA to tap our full potential. I believe what you sent me could be the missing link or at least a significant piece of the puzzle. Even though the sample you sent me was no longer alive, my findings would suggest that it had amazing adaptive power."

After a second long pause, Allan said, "Well yes, that is quite interesting."

"Quite interesting? That might just be the greatest understatement in the history of science!" Lionel replied. "That would be like people telling Copernicus when he postulated that the sun was the center of our solar system, 'That's quite interesting', or when Einstein explained the theory of relativity, the rest of the world saying, 'That's interesting.'"

"Well, it is interesting. Hell, what do you want me to say?"

"I want you to tell me where the specimen came from," Lionel replied.

"I can't do that," Allan said.

There was another long pause on the other end of the line.

"Then just answer me this one question. There was a rumor floating around among some of my fellow researchers a while back. I don't remember the details exactly since I try to ignore rumors, but I do recall something about some scientist making available what he was calling the modeling clay of life. The story goes that the feds found out about it and shut it all down. I was just wondering if you knew anything about that?"

"Just sounds like another one of those crazy conspiracy theories," Allan replied. "I wouldn't give it any credence."

"That's what I thought as well," Lionel agreed, "until I received your package. You know, someone told me once that not all conspiracy theories are false. What if this one were true?"

"I wouldn't know anything about that," Allan lied. "Listen, I really need to go."

"Okay, okay. I get it. You don't want to talk. Just answer one other question; yes or no. Is it from this planet?"

Do I dare answer that question? Allan thought. After all, it wasn't like he was talking to a total stranger. He and Lionel went back decades. That's why he had finally decided to send the larva to him. If he couldn't trust an old friend like Lionel with the truth, who could he trust?

"No," Adam finally replied. "It's not of this Earth, and that's all I'll say about it. Do with it as you will, but be very careful with it, and please, don't ever tell anyone where you got it. Promise me that."

"Sure, if that's what you want," Lionel replied.

"That's what I want," Allan said. "And while I have appreciated you calling me and giving me this update, I'd really like us to consider the subject closed."

"Are you sure? I'll be happy to..."

"Yes, I'm sure. Thanks for calling." Allan hung up the phone but continued to sit at this desk for several minutes staring at the phone mulling over the conversation. *Amazing adaptive powers. My old friend doesn't know the half of it.*

Val's New Home

1

Aeo studied the outfit he'd fabricated from the skin of the bear. It would only fit Val for a couple of weeks at best, but that would be enough time for him to become established in the human's society where he could acquire more appropriate clothes.

He'd gotten the idea while surfing the internet and stumbled upon the cultural phenomenon of Teddy bears which epitomized the cuteness and innocence of young humans. He calculated that it would increase Val's chances of finding a suitable first home if he looked as cute and cuddly as possible.

He had Val try on the outfit then studied the boy. Perhaps the bear ears was a little much he thought but finally decided to keep them. After all, humans, particularly female humans seemed to eat up such displays of cuteness.

"Tomorrow will be the day you leave the security of the cave to resume your mission, so let's review the relevant data one last time."

Val nodded. "Can I take this off first? It's hot and itchy."

"Yes," Aeo replied. "But tomorrow you will need to wear it until you've made contact with the appropriate humans who will see how hot and itchy it is and will provide you with more appropriate clothing. *At least that's the plan,* Aeo thought.

"Now, what is the name you are to tell humans?"

"Val."

"And what is your real name that you must not reveal but also never forget?"

"Sluneg," the boy replied.

2

THE WINDING MOUNTAIN road was not well traveled. Aeo had intentionally selected it for that very reason. On its excursions around the area and from his research, he deducted that larger roads with more traffic also increased the risk of Val being picked up by a dangerous human, of which there were plenty. But this road was traveled mostly by the local mountain folks. Val had been instructed to look for a middle-aged or older couple, ideally a husband and wife, or if a couple didn't come along, two older females, but the vehicle must have at least one woman, Aeo stressed since it would greatly increase his chances of integrating into a hospitable environment.

It didn't take long before the perfect subjects arrived driving a rust-colored sedan. The man behind the wheel had gray, almost white hair, as did the woman who sat in the seat beside him. They were driving well under the speed limit which gave Val an extra few seconds to make his decision. As the car slowed even further to round the sharp curve in the road, Val stepped out of his hiding place and waved. *Remember, cute and cuddly...cute and cuddly.*

3

HAROLD AND MAUDE JOHNSON traveled this way at least twice a month to visit their daughter and two grandkids that lived in Foster Flat three mountains over. Maude glanced over at her husband of forty years, his two hands firmly gripping the wheel at ten and two staring straight ahead. While she appreciated how safe a driver her husband was, which allowed him to keep his driver's license well into his seventies, she did wish at times he would drive faster than thirty miles an hour. After all, he knew this road as well as he knew the winding veins that coursed along the back of his hand, but whenever she tried to gently nudge him to increase his speed, the reply was always the same.

"You never know what unexpected thing might pop up on these roads. Might be a downed tree from a recent thunderstorm, or a wreck from someone less careful." If she persisted, his last reply would always win. "I'd be happy to turn the driving over to you if you don't care for my safety ways."

She sometimes wondered if she took him up on the offer whether he'd actually pull over and let her take the wheel. She suspected not, but no matter. One didn't stay more or less happily married for four-plus decades by picking such senseless fights. "Choose your battles if you want to win the war," her mom had told her the night before she married Harold. It had been the only advice she'd given the young bride, but it had served her well over the years. This was one battle not worth fighting. She glanced out the window as Harold slowed even further to make the hairpin turn in the road.

What was that on the side of the road? A bear cub? Couldn't be. Bear cubs didn't wave as you drove by.

"What in the world was that?" Harold asked, at the same moment slowing even further.

"Can you pull over?" Maude asked reaching out and clutching Harold's arm.

"Not safe to pull over on these mountain roads..." Harold began.

"Please," Maude insisted, craning her neck to look behind her.

"Oh, okay, I guess. What was that thing, anyway?"

"I'm not sure," Maude replied, "but I think it might have been a little boy dressed up like a bear."

"Out here? There's not a house within five miles!"

"I know."

"You stay in the car, and I'll check it out," Harold said as he unclipped his seatbelt and looked behind him to be sure the road was clear.

"Not on your life," Maude replied, releasing her own seatbelt and opening her car door before he had time to stop her. And then there were battles worth fighting.

4

VAL WATCHED AS THE automobile slowed to pull off the road. Had Aeo's plan worked on his first try? Apparently so. *Cute and cuddly,* he reminded himself one last time then smiled and waved again as the two elderly humans exited their vehicle and started walking towards them, the old man frowning while the woman smiled warmly. So it was true what Aeo had told him. The females were more susceptible to cute and cuddly than the males.

The woman reached him first. When she approached within a few yards, Val let out a soft whimper and forced a tear from both eyes. Aeo had pointed out to him that cute and cuddly could take on many different forms, and that tears and crying could be particularly effective under the right conditions.

"Help me," Val said, his lower lip quivering.

"Oh, you poor thing," the woman replied walking over to him and bending down to his level. "What in the world are you doing out here in the middle of nowhere? Where are your parents?" *Val remembered* Aeo had instructed him *not to answer questions if he didn't know the answer, or if he preferred not to respond.*

The first question didn't make sense to him. He wasn't in the middle of nowhere. He knew exactly where he was. He could have told the woman his exact location, even the exact distance from the cave that had been his home for the past months. As to the second question, Aeo had warned him about any reference to parents, or mothers, or fathers.

"Help me...please." He whimpered again, louder this time. He held out his arms, inviting the woman to approach, which she did, scooping him up in her arms and hugging him.

Could manipulating humans be so easy? Evidently so.

Hunting Wolf

I t started off innocently enough. Late one Thursday, Mimi, Kendra, and TJ were sitting around Allan's office, which doubled as TJ's homeschool room, after a lengthy study session. Kendra had called for a short break when Mimi spoke up.

"Did you hear about the wolf on old man Elbertson's land?"

"What? No," Kendra replied. "Really? I thought wolves were extinct in these parts."

"Yeah, that's what makes it so interesting," Mimi replied. "My Uncle Bo told me about it this morning at breakfast. He did say that Elbertson sometimes gets into the moonshine a bit too heavily, so he wasn't sure how true it was. Still, Elbertson claims he's been on the wagon for months and that he saw a red wolf with his own eyes on his land. That's not far from here."

"On the wagon?" TJ asked, his interest suddenly piqued.

"It means he's not been drinking any moonshine or other alcohol," Mimi explained. "Every few years someone reports seeing a red wolf in the area, but it never amounts to anything. They used to be fairly common around these parts many years ago, but not anymore."

"Where is Elbertson's?" TJ asked.

"Just to the north of Dr. Pritchard's land. I'd say it's only a mile or two away," Kendra replied. "But you stay away from there. Allan would freak out if he knew you'd gone over there."

"Oh, sure," TJ replied, *but then again, what he doesn't know won't hurt him,* he thought. If there really was a wolf on Elbertson's land, he wanted to see it. TJ could hardly wait until the weekend when he'd have a chance to slip away and investigate the rumor. Over the next two days he continued to think about how to go about meeting a wolf, and by Saturday he had his plan laid out.

TJ had continued to think about being able to shapeshift into different animal forms. His research on the internet had revealed that wolves and dogs were closely akin to each other. It made sense that since he already knew how to shift into a dog form, it shouldn't be all that difficult to become a wolf. His research had also uncovered that one of the best ways to attract a predator was to mimic the sound of an injured rabbit. The website even had a recording of the sound, which TJ had practiced until he had it down perfectly, but would he be able to replicate it in his canine form?

The first several times he tried to produce the high pitch squealing noise it had come out sounding more like a wounded moose than a rabbit. His vocal chords had definitely changed along with the rest of him. He continued to work on it until the sound slowly came around. He recalled the warning that had been on the website:

"The rabbit squeal is a call that works anywhere in the world, and has the potential to bring in anything from a bobcat to a grizzly bear, but be fair warned: you're ringing the dinner bell and whatever comes in is hungry and looking for a quick meal."

I think it would be far better to be in the form of a large dog than a human if my plan actually does work, he thought, as he started trotting in the direction of Elbertson's farm. He reached the border between the two lands in less than twenty minutes. He stood gazing at the old fence that was in need of repair that separated Allan's property from Elbertson's. He had wandered out this far a few times before but had always stopped upon reaching the border. It felt strange knowing that today he'd go beyond. He glanced around, half expecting to see someone spying on him just waiting for him to break his promise, but he saw no one. He was alone in the middle of the woods, as he'd been countless times before. Besides it being a neat idea to be able to become a wolf, there were some advantages to the shape. Wolves' chests and hips were proportionately narrower than dogs. This, coupled with the fact that wolves' legs were longer with larger paws, allowed them to run long distances at very high speeds. They were also known to be good hunters and able to survive in the wild either in packs or alone.

Slipping away had been easy. Everyone was accustomed to him spending several hours hiking through the woods surrounding his home. This time he'd just have to roam a little further. He also had found a spot to stash his clothes that was easy to find again. He went there now, undressed, and as quickly as possible shifted into his canine form.

He took a running start and easily cleared the fence where the top board had broken down from age and was surprised by the adrenalin rush he felt at breaking free. He trotted off into the new woods, which looked and felt just like the ones he'd just left. He continued on until he reached the crest of a hill that overlooked Elbertson's homestead; a log home much like the one he lived in and two outbuildings: a barn and henhouse. According to the paper, Elbertson had claimed the wolf had been attracted to the homestead because of the hens, and it had been the hens' squawking that had drawn Elbertson outside to investigate. That's when he'd seen the wolf. It seemed to be the best place to start his search, but what if Elbertson saw him and thought he was the wolf returning? According to Mimi, old man Elbertson not only enjoyed his share of moonshine but over the years his eyesight had grown worse. The last thing he needed was for an old drunkard to mistake him for a wolf and end up shooting him.

TJ stood on the edge of the forest, uncertain whether to proceed. The breeze shifted, and suddenly he detected a new smell; one that he'd never smelled before but instantly identified very much like his own odor. *It must be that of the wolf,* he thought. Maybe he didn't need to go any further. He'd just follow the scent and see where it took him. He lifted his nose in the air and took another whiff. Yes, there it was again. It seemed to be coming from his left, so he headed off in that direction, staying just inside the perimeter of the forest for cover. The scent led him to travel more deeply in the woods. Now he kept his nose close to the ground where the scent was strongest. He had the wolf's trail. *It won't be long now,* he thought just before he reached the creek where the trail ended.

He traveled up and down the creek bed, trying to pick up the scent again, but without any luck. Now, what was he to do? He was in the middle of nowhere without a clue which direction to go. That's when he remembered the rabbit squeal. What did he have to lose? He might as well try it, but what if it ended up attracting some other predator? He figured he could handle himself if the squeal attracted a bobcat, but what about a bear? He wasn't so sure. Still, he had come all this way to find and meet a wolf. He wasn't about to go home without trying everything he could think of to fulfill his mission.

He trotted along the creek bed until he found a good place where he could burrow down behind a fallen tree. As he hid as best he could, he recalled the other bit of information from the website: "When out in the field trying it out, don't call too often. Less is more in these situations. The more you call, the more likely you are to be busted. Animals like coyotes, for instance, are opportunistic hunters, meaning they will be easily drawn into such a sound, but calling too often will turn their curiosity into caution."

Okay, I'll try it a few times, wait a couple minutes and try again. If nothing happens, I'll call it a day and go home. He sat there for a moment imagining what it would feel like to be a wounded rabbit in pain. *May as well get into the role,* he thought. When he felt like he had a grasp of being a rabbit, he cleared his throat and squealed three of four times. It sent a chill up his spine. It sure sounded like an injured animal to him. He waited a couple of minutes, listening for any sound of an approaching animal, but all he heard was the breeze rustling the few remaining leaves that were still on the trees.

He tried a second time, squealing a little more urgently and waited again. Still nothing. *I guess I don't make as good a rabbit as I thought.* He was just about to call it quits and go home when he heard a different rustle off to his left. He held his breath and waited until he heard the sound again, this time closer. Something was coming towards him. Should he raise his head and look? What if he came face to face with a bear? What would he do? *Stop pretending to be a wounded rabbit and run like hell,* he answered his own question.

Then the rustling of the approaching animal stopped. Had it picked up his scent and run off? Only one way to find out. Taking a deep breath, he slowly raised his head and looked in the direction of the sound and came face to face with the red wolf standing only ten feet away. The two stared at each other for a second that seemed to stretch out into minutes, both startled by the other. It was the wolf who broke first, running into the thick brush of the woods. TJ stood up to give chase but then stopped. The wolf was faster and could run farther than he could. He'd come out here to see if there was such an animal and not just a figment of an old drunkard's vivid imagination. He'd confirmed its existence. Now what?

What had Homlin told him? To become a new form, you need a sample of that form. It hadn't made much sense to him at the time. After all, he'd been much younger, but since then he'd done his own research, trying to figure out Homlin's meaning. He thought he'd found the answer in the field of genetics. The key to becoming an animal, be it a human, mammal, bird or whatever, was within each and every cell of that species body hidden away in its DNA. To become a wolf, he would need a sample of the wolf. *But what if I can't get the wolf to slow down long enough for that?*

Wolves lived in dens, which were often abandoned holes of other animals. Maybe he could find this wolf's den, and maybe, just maybe, there'd be some part of the wolf left behind that he could use to begin the assimilation process. So, instead of heading in the direction the wolf had run, TJ sniffed around until he picked up the scent of where the wolf had traveled from. Sure enough, it eventually led him back to a hole in the ground where the scent of wolf was strong—very strong, but there was another smell that competed with the wolf's scent; a strong, pungent smell of death.

TJ could feel the hackles on his back. Both scents came from the entryway of the den, so TJ lowered himself and crawled forward. The opening was just barely large enough for the wolf and too small for TJ's large canine form. However, he could get his head and part of his neck into it. Whatever it was inside was just beyond his reach. He waited for his eyes to adjust to the subdued light. Slowly, he could just make out a small form. Was it a rabbit? No, he'd smelled rabbits before while traipsing around in the woods, and he couldn't detect anything like that. In fact, the only animal scent he could identify was that of the wolf. He pushed himself further into the hole. Just another inch or two and he could reach the still form with his mouth and drag it out.

Meanwhile, the human part of him felt like it would vomit from the smell. *I'm glad I skipped breakfast this morning,* he thought. *It would certainly be all over the place by now.* He took another deep breath, then let it out, trying to shrink his body just a little more. It worked. He felt himself slide forward just enough to grasp the small form. As soon as he had it in his mouth, he backed out of the hole and into the light of day. He dropped the object on the ground and stepped back in shock. It was the decaying carcass of a wolf pup.

He turned away, spitting and gagging in disgust.

Be careful what you wish for because you might just get it. It was one of Kendra's favorite sayings that had never made much sense to TJ...until now. He stared down at the small body of the decaying wolf pup. *How do I know this whole crazy scheme of mine will even work?* Homlin hadn't been all that specific or clear about the process. Just that it helped tremendously to have some part of the form you wanted to assimilate into. And there it was before him, but what was he supposed to do with it? Would it be sufficient to rub it on his dog form? He decided to give it a try. Holding his breath, he nuzzled the partially decomposed carcass, then rubbed his head and neck on it, coming away once again gagging and now smelling like rotten meat.

That's not going to work, he thought. *All I've managed to do is make myself smell so bad I'll be banned from ever entering Allan's home again.* No, he knew what he'd have to do if he had any hope of becoming a wolf. Whatever ability he had to shift from one form to another was not on his skin or fur. It was deep within him. If he were truly committed to adding wolf form to his repertoire, he'd have to take a sample of wolf inside him and the only way he knew to do that was to eat the damn putrid thing. Eat it and then pray he had a strong enough stomach to keep it down so his digestive system could absorb the all-important DNA.

He could feel an inner battle taking place. His canine aspect didn't find the idea all that abhorrent while the human aspect made him gag for the third time. After he finished, a thought came to him. If his canine aspect could stomach the idea of devouring the wolf pup maybe he just needed to wait a while until that part of him took over, then after finishing the task, quickly shift back to human form long enough to become comfortable in that form once again. He could then jog home as a human or shift back to the dog form.

Is it really that important to learn to become a wolf? Maybe he could start with some other form? How about a chicken? He liked chicken and ate it several times a week. Maybe he already had that raw material to make such a shift. So what? Who in the hell wants to become a chicken and end up on someone else's dinner plate? And for sure, becoming a wolf would have much more practical use when he later became a mercenary for hire. And that's what this was really about, more than the coolness of being a wolf, there was the practical aspect of it as well.

He could just imagine some terrorist like Song in the mercenary game thinking he'd gotten a jump on TJ the Merc, only to watch as his victim suddenly transformed into a hungry wolf. Yea! Wolves ruled!

TJ studied the putrid carcass. Maybe wolves ruled, but at the moment his human nature was still a little too strong. He walked away before the gagging started again. His plan was risky; no question about it. If he waited too long, he might forget his human form, and he'd be stuck as an oversized Saint Bernard for the rest of his life. But the life of a Merc would be risky as well. He may as well start getting used to taking risks.

It took him a good twenty minutes before he could walk over to the carcass of the wolf pup and sniff it without gagging, and another thirty minutes before he felt his canine aspect strong enough to try biting into it. But once he started, he was determined to eat as much as he could before the gag reflex took over. After all, even dogs had their limits. He managed to get half of it down before he felt it starting to come back up.

That's it. That will have to be enough, he thought as he backed away from the remains. As he retraced his steps to the stream, he prayed that he'd not just made a fool of himself. Upon reaching the creek, he lapped up as much water as he could hold to wash the taste of rotted meat from his mouth. He just about had his fill when he saw a flicker of motion off to his left. He jerked his head up in time to see a rabbit bounding away. *Fresh rabbit would taste far better than rotten wolf,* he thought as he took out after the cottontail. Time to find out if they really made that squealing noise. Where had he heard it? He couldn't remember, and it didn't seem all that important. His one and only objective at this point was to catch that damn rabbit.

Lost Dog

1

Rabbits were fast; far faster than he was. He'd have to find his next meal somewhere else, but where? He couldn't remember what besides rabbit he ate. There was that putrid wolf pup, but his stomach hadn't handled that very well. It would be better to stay with food that was fresher in the future. The rabbit had really sent him on a wild chase through the woods. By the time he figured out that he'd never catch the damn thing, he was far from the creek, and it was starting to get dark.

Time to head for home, he thought, then stopped. Home? Where was home? He couldn't remember. Surely, he had someplace that he stayed; somewhere that he slept at the end of the day. Home is where the heart is. What was that supposed to mean? He felt like he had heard that before, but he couldn't imagine where. His mind seemed more muddled than usual, and his memory was virtually nonexistent. He remembered drinking from the creek, the rabbit chase and his attempt to eat the putrid wolf pup, but that was about it. Surely there was more to his past than that. Think. Where had he slept the night before?

As he pondered the question, an image popped into his awareness and along with it a name — Allan. And in the next instant a second image of a log house. Home. Where he'd slept the night before. Allan must be his, or perhaps it was more accurate to say that he was Allan's. In either case, he felt sure Allan would give him something to eat that would taste much better than a putrid wolf pup, and maybe even as good as that rascal rabbit.

It took him close to an hour to figure out which direction home was. During that time he wandered around, occasionally stopping to sniff the air. He felt certain that he'd recognize the home smell once he got close enough to it and he was right. Once sniffed, never forgotten. He headed in the direction of home.

By the time he had the log house in his view, his appetite had grown, and the nauseous feeling of earlier had disappeared. But as he approached the house something didn't feel right. Had he somehow stumbled upon the wrong place? No. The house looked the same and smelled just as he remembered it, but something about his approach felt foreign. He slowed his pace as he drew nearer, a feeling of foreboding slowly mounting as the front porch came in sight. Then the front door opened and out stepped Allan—his alpha dog. Surely he was home after all. As he trotted up the steps to lick Allan's hand, he swore he'd never eat putrid wolf pup ever again.

2

"MOLLIE? IS THAT YOU?" Allan asked as he took a step towards the large dog that was trotting towards him. The dog looked a lot like the Parker's pregnant bitch that he'd performed a C-section on over a year ago, but this dog was even larger and a male, but given how friendly the dog was acting, it must be one of his patients. The dog bounded up the stairs straight towards him, almost knocking him over as it jumped up on him, the two large paws hitting him squarely in the chest.

"Whoa, boy. Down. Behave yourself," Allan said as he grabbed the two paws and placed them firmly back on the ground. "Who are you, boy? Are you lost? Where's your owner?" But even as he asked the questions, he was afraid he already knew the answers. This wasn't Mollie, but it was her lone surviving pup. The one that he'd taken home that evening and raised not to be a puppy, but to become his son.

"TJ? Is that you? God, you smell awful. What in the world happened?" And how in the hell would he ever explain this to Kendra who was still inside waiting for TJ, the human, to return from his weekend romp in the woods?

"Come on, boy, we've got to get you out of sight fast." He grabbed the large dog by the loose skin at the scruff of its neck and guided him to the storage building in the backyard. The dog seemed so happy to see him that he willingly went with Allan.

"I'm sorry, boy, but you'll need to stay here for just a little while. As soon as I get rid of Kendra, I'll come back out and..." And what? What in the hell would he do then? He'd have to figure that one out a little later. First, he had to send Kendra on her way.

3

ALLAN HAD SUSPECTED all along that TJ could turn himself back into dog form. After all, he'd seen the boy's footprints change to those of a dog when he'd run away from home and had later turned up at Homlin's preserve. Those suspicions were now confirmed, but something else must be going on. Why would TJ run the risk of being discovered in this way by returning home in his canine form...unless he had become stuck in that form?

In which case it was up to Allan to help him remember his true form, which would take time. Allan started by calling his receptionist.

"I know this is spur of the moment, but I'm going away for a few days. Please reschedule my appointments and contact Dr. Wade across town and ask him to check on my cases. I've done it for him a few times, so he owes me a favor. Also, let Kendra know I won't need her until I return."

"Are you okay?" Donna asked.

"Yeah, I'm fine. I'll be in touch," Allan said and then hung up to avoid any other questions.

Now at least I have a little time to figure this out, he thought. He knew Pat was attending a conference in Nashville and wouldn't be back until at least the middle of next week. That gave him three or four days to help TJ remember.

After bathing the dog to remove the putrid odor, he brought the giant dog in from the storage room and placed him back in TJ's bedroom.

"This is your room, TJ. Remember?" Allan spoke as though talking directly to his son, though it felt odd doing so. He watched as the dog sniffed around the room, stopping at each piece of furniture. *I just hope he doesn't decide to claim his territory by lifting his leg on everything,* Allan thought, chuckling.

"Are you hungry, boy...I mean TJ?" Allan corrected himself. "I'll fix us some dinner in just a little while." But first, it was essential to start the imprinting process that he'd used before and pray it would work again.

He went throughout the house collecting every picture he could find of his son, Todd, and the few pictures he had of TJ he'd started keeping a photo album. He placed them around TJ's room on every flat surface. "This is you, TJ. I think you may have forgotten, but this is your true form. You're human. Remember?"

The dog sat in the middle of the floor and looked at him, cocking its head from side to side.

"Remember? This is your room. You're my son. You enjoy eating Cheerios by the boxful, and...and Kendra and Mimi are your friends. You must remember them, right?"

But the dog continued to stare at him, cocking his head and whining softly.

Oh boy, this isn't going to be easy, Allan thought. And what if this wasn't TJ after all? What if this was just some stray dog with a particularly friendly disposition and TJ was out there in the woods, maybe hurt or worse?

No, I can't start doubting myself now. If I want TJ to remember his true form, I have to start by believing that this is him, and doing everything I can to help him. He squared his shoulders and went to see if he could find any other pictures, and on the way through the kitchen stopped and poured a big bowl of Cheerios, which he took back to feed to the dog.

This continued for the next three days without any sign it was working. Allan even debated calling Kendra to come over and help but decided against it. She'd been so understanding of TJ's rapid growth, but he was pretty sure she'd freak out to learn of the boy's shapeshifting abilities.

On the third night, Allan stepped into TJ's room to find the dog sleeping on the floor. Allan looked around the room at the dozens of photos of TJ at different ages. As far as he could tell, the dog hadn't paid the first iota of attention to them. Noticing the door to TJ's closet, he entered the walk-in closet to see if he could find anything else that might initiate the remembering process, but all he found was the clutter of a young boy; shoes were strewn around as well as a pile of old clothes in need of washing.

It struck him as funny that a boy could do such a good job of maintaining a clean bedroom but that the habit didn't extend to his closet. He'd have to remember to bundle up the dirty clothes and wash them tomorrow before they started to mildew.

As he returned to the bedroom, Allan noticed the dog was awake and was staring at him, its tail slowly wagging. He walked over and sat down beside it and rubbed behind its ear. "What are we going to do, TJ? Am I going to lose you for a second time and have to settle for a loyal canine companion?"

And how would he explain all this to Pat, who was due to arrive tomorrow afternoon? Talk about someone freaking out. This would likely be the last straw for her. Allan continued to sit with the dog for several minutes before finally standing up.

"Okay, TJ. Sleep well. I'll see you in the morning."

The dog thumped its tail on the carpet and rested its massive head on its paws.

4

AFTER THE FRIENDLY man had left, the dog continued to lie on the floor, dozing off and on. He wished the man had thought to bring him another bowl of those sweet, crispy treats, but he guessed he'd have to wait until morning for more.

He lifted his head and looked around on the off chance he'd missed a crumb or two even though he knew better. As he did so, his eyes fell on the second door that the man had used earlier and left cracked open. *Wonder what's in there? Could there be something good to eat? Worth checking out.* He slowly stood up and stretched before walking over to the closet door. He nuzzled it open with his nose and stepped inside, taking a couple deep breaths in the hopes of smelling the sweet treats or anything else to satisfy his hunger pangs, but he didn't detect anything edible. He did, however, pick up the pungent odor of another human. He lowered his head and sniffed at the pile of clothes. Yep, there it was...strong...and strangely familiar. Did he know this other human? It felt like he did, or at least that he should recognize him. In fact, the smell was so strong and so familiar he couldn't understand why he couldn't put a face or a name...wait. Suddenly a face did pop before him. One he'd seen for the past few days all around him. This pile must belong to the boy in the pictures, and now he remembered he liked that boy very much.

He stepped onto the pile and circled around. Yes, the boy was his friend. Maybe more than a friend. He circled around one last time before lying down. As he closed his eyes, he remembered the boy's name; TJ. Yeah, that was right.

TJ, but hadn't that been what the man had called him over and over? How could he and the boy have the same name...unless...?

The dog drifted off to sleep dreaming about TJ and he playing together, wrestling on the ground like two pups from the same litter. As they continued to roll around, the two forms became one.

Aunt Maggie

Dropping my two girls off at my sister, Maggie's home is the most difficult part of my second profession, James thought, as he pulled the white service van to the curb in front of her house.

"All right, girls, remember to not give Aunt Maggie a hard time. Do what she says and no complaining. I don't want to receive a report from her like the last time.

"Aunt Maggie is such a tattletale," Melissa Jean, the older one, whispered to her sister.

"I heard that," James turned in his seat to give her a stern look.

"Well, she is."

"I like Aunt Maggie," Melissa Jean said.

"That's because she lets you stay up as late as I do which really isn't fair either. I'm older."

"So? That's doesn't mean anything."

"Now girls, no fighting. Give me a hug. I'm going to miss you," James said as he opened the van door and stepped around to retrieve the girls' luggage.

As the three of them took the familiar walk up the sidewalk to his sister's house, James thanked the heavens one more time for his sister's generous nature. She had never prodded about what James' second business involved, though he suspected she knew it wasn't completely above board, she'd been a godsend.

It had been one of Jenny's last good ideas she'd shared with him on her deathbed at the hospice.

"You know Margaret loves our kids as though they were her own, and since she'll never be able to have her own children, letting her help out would be a double blessing," Jenny had said in that soft voice of hers. It had been one of Jenny's favorite pastimes, looking for and finding *double blessings*. She'd certainly found a gem with this one.

As James and the girls approached, the large red door swung open, and Aunt Maggie stood beaming at them.

"And there are my two favorite little people in all the world...oh, and my dearly, demented brother as well. Off for how long this time?"

"Not sure," James replied as he handed one of the suitcases to his sister. "But shouldn't be as long as the last business meeting. No more than a week, I wouldn't think."

Maggie nodded. James noticed her smile flicker into a momentary frown as she leaned over and kissed him on the cheek. "Well, take good care of yourself. It's a dangerous world out there."

It had become her parting phrase whenever he had to leave his two most precious girls with her. He suspected it was her way of letting him know that she never bought the stories that his business trips were to conferences about heating and air conditioning. It was the closest they ever came to discussing what these trips were really about, and he loved his sister all the more for not prying nor judging him.

Found

1

As Allan slowly awoke, he remembered what day it was and what he'd been struggling with for the past three days. He groaned and thought seriously of pulling the covers over his head and going back to sleep, but he knew he'd not be able to return to dreamland. He had work to do and time was running out. Pat would be back in town later in the afternoon.

He walked into the bathroom to relieve himself, then threw some cold water on his face to help him wake up before walking into the kitchen to start a fresh pot of coffee. As the coffee was brewing, he pulled a fresh box of Cheerios out of the cabinet and filled a bowl with the cereal. As he walked to the other end of the house towards TJ's room, he could feel a blanket of resignation weighing him down. Maybe it was best this way, he thought, even though he didn't believe it. As a large dog, TJ could go pretty much anywhere he wanted and be accepted just as he was. Certainly, that wasn't the case as a rapidly growing human. He'd always be an outcast and someone who Allan would have to hide away.

He stopped outside TJ's bedroom door and stared down at the bowl of cereal. *Get a hold of yourself. You can't lose faith. You've got to keep trying. Maybe by some miracle, something would happen to delay Pat so he'd have more time. Yeah, that's it. Maybe he could come up with some excuse to keep Pat away for at least another day or two, but how much longer could he expect Dr. Wade to cover his cases and Donna to keep putting off his regular clients?*

Okay, one step at a time. Give the pup his morning treat and let him out. One step at a time. Allan squared his shoulders once again, preparing himself as best he could to relate to the large dog as his lost son, but when he entered the room, there was no sign of the dog. Had he crawled under the bed? A quick search turned up negative. Then he noticed the door to the closet was open. He must have forgotten to close it the night before.

He walked over and opened it to find TJ curled up asleep on the pile of dirty clothes. He smiled, then chuckled, then broke out into a full laugh as he looked down at the naked body of his son.

2

EVEN THOUGH IT WAS the summer months when most schools were out, TJ continued his homeschooling, taking advantage of the extra time that Kendra and Mimi had available. It didn't bother him that all the other kids in the area were on summer break. He loved to learn, and he particularly enjoyed having Mimi as his teacher. When they weren't studying, the three of them also enjoyed playing *Mercenaries*. TJ had even developed a long distance relationship with one of the game's programmers, offering suggestions for future editions of the game. TJ not only pointed out bugs in the program but offered several fixes that amazed the game's originator.

But now summer was drawing to a close, and next week Kendra and Mimi would be returning to school. *That's okay*, TJ thought. *I'll still be able to see Mimi most afternoons, as well as on weekends.* He even played with the idea of showing her his shapeshifting abilities that had continued to improve with practice. He could now morph not only into a dog and wolf but also into a great grey owl, though he was still mastering the ability to fly in that form.

So, TJ was stunned when Mimi delivered the news.

"I'm really sorry to have to tell you this with such short notice, but my dad laid down the law about my almost failing last year, and he's even gotten Uncle Bo to go along with his decision."

"What decision is that?" Kendra asked. The three of them were sitting in Allan's office.

"He told me that I can't continue to come over here and help with TJ's homeschooling," Mimi replied with a quiver in her voice.

"What?" TJ asked. He'd only been half listening with the rest of his attention on booting up the computer. "What did you just say?"

"I'm afraid that this is the last week I'll be able to come over and help you with your studies," Mimi repeated.

"I'm sorry to hear that," Kendra said as she stood up and walked over to give her friend a consolatory hug. "You've been so much help this summer, but I'm sure TJ and I will manage. Your studies have to come first. After all, we can't have a future Pulitzer Prize winner flunking out of school."

"Yes we can," TJ said as he jumped out of his chair and took a step towards the two girls. "I mean, of course, your school work is important, but you can't stop coming over. I can help you with your studies. Tit for tat or something like that."

"That's sweet, TJ, and I appreciate it, but you don't know my father. He seldom pays any attention to his daughter, but when he gets something in his mind like this, there's no changing it."

Mimi walked over to TJ, her arms outstretched to give him a hug as well, but before she reached him, he angrily turned away. How many times in the past had he imagined the two of them locked in a loving embrace, even kissing passionately? But not now, not after this news. He stormed out of the room.

"Where are you going?" Kendra called after him.

"None of your business!" he shouted over his shoulder as he grabbed his jacket. He flung the door open and ran across the porch, taking the steps in one giant leap. Hitting the ground at full velocity, he ran away, picking up speed with every step, ignoring the calls from Kendra and Mimi.

In the past months TJ had grown from a young adolescent into a handsome teenage boy that could have easily passed for any of Kendra or Mimi's schoolmates, so now as he ran through the woods, he felt the sinewy muscles of his body as he called for more speed. Had it only been his imagination? Had he misread the signs in the past few weeks that had led him to believe that Mimi had feelings for him as he had for her? Or maybe she had just been leading him on. Having a lot of fun with their weird kid that grew too fast. Hell, she was probably just playing them along so she could gather more information to include in her damn book.

As he ran through the woods, cutting back and forth to avoid the trees in his path, his anger grew, and he could feel his body demanding to turn, but into what? Did it matter, as long as it wasn't his human form? As he ran, he tossed off his clothes, finally stopping just long enough to remove his jeans, kicking off his shoes at the same time. Maybe he would turn himself into the dog form, then wait for Mimi to leave on her bike and attack her. Or how about shapeshifting into a great gray owl so he could fly above her, and sink his sharp talons into her neck? The thoughts just added fuel to his anger and he felt the transformation begin but not into a dog nor into an owl, but into another form he didn't recognize, though it felt so right.

He could remember seeing a similar form only once before, and even then it was mixed with the human form known as Homlin. But how was it possible that he, TJ, could be taking on a form that he'd only seen once and never practiced? Could it be that Pat was correct? Was he truly an alien and the TJ form merely a disguise? Imagine showing up on the path that Mimi took when she rode her bicycle home in this form. Would she even recognize him as the young kid she'd spent her summer teaching and leaning on? The hell with her. It was time to start looking out for number one, and he was hungry. One of the things he knew about this form was that it was the perfect killing machine. And if this was who he indeed was underneath all the façade of being human, he may as well use it to satisfy his needs.

He had only just had that thought when he caught the familiar whiff of a deer in the air and almost as quickly knew which direction and how far away it was. Yes, this form would come in mighty handy. He changed the direction he was running and headed towards the deer.

Tracking

1

As Pat drove down the bumpy winding road to Allan's home, she thought for about the twentieth time that they really should have someone come out to fill in the potholes and grade it, but even as she had the thought, she knew it was unlikely that Allan would agree to it. After all, that would be one other person who might discover TJ's secret, and the last thing she needed to do right now was to create any more waves in their tenuous relationship. At the same time she had to admit that since TJ's birthday, things had been going more smoothly. Of course, some of that could be credited to the fact that she was still spending a lot of her time in Charlotte, but when she did return, they had managed to find a way to get along. She had done the best she could over the past several weeks to treat TJ as the others were treating him, and so far it was working.

As she took the last bend in the road, she could see the log home coming into view through the trees. *It feels good to be home,* she thought. Home? Was this her home? Or was the apartment in Charlotte her home and this just a place she visited frequently? She was still contemplating the questions when she saw a flash of motion as TJ streaked across the porch, took a flying leap off the steps and across the yard, followed closely by Kendra and Mimi. Were they playing a game of tag, Pat wondered? Seeing the look of anger on TJ's face and the distress on the faces of the two girls she doubted they were playing.

Pat pulled her car into her customary parking space, quickly turned it off, and jumped out to see if she could help, but by the time she got out of the car, TJ had already disappeared into the woods.

"What's going on here?" Pat called to the two girls as she trotted towards them. "Is everything alright? Where is TJ going?"

Kendra turned around to look at her with an exasperated look on her face. As the two of them walked towards each other Kendra waved her arms up and down in frustration. "Mimi's father ordered her to stop helping TJ with his homeschooling so she could focus on her studies instead. TJ didn't take the news very well."

Oh shit, Pat thought. *Now I've gone and done it.* She had forgotten about calling Mimi's father several weeks ago when things weren't going well between TJ and her. She'd also noticed the crush TJ was developing on Mimi, and she didn't like it; didn't like it at all. So, she had decided to do something about it. Obviously, the phone call had worked.

Realizing she was the cause of this current upset, it was up to her to try and fix it. "You girls go back inside," Pat said. "I'll go find TJ and bring him home. Try not to worry. He'll settle down in a little while."

Kendra and Mimi did as they were told, and Pat started off in the direction she'd last seen TJ running. *Time to brush up on my old tracking skills,* Pat thought as she followed the footprints through the woods. Luckily it had rained just the day before, leaving the ground soft, plus TJ certainly wasn't trying to hide his tracks. She could even hear him rustling through the thick undergrowth of the forest from time to time.

That's okay, TJ, Pat thought. *You go ahead and run off your anger. You may have speed on your side, but I have time on mine.* She occasionally paused to listen and study the terrain. She thought about calling out to him but then thought better of it, fearful that it might alarm him that someone was following him. Best to just let him calm down a little first.

As she trotted up a steep hill, she glanced at her watch. She figured she'd been following him for close to thirty minutes and she hoped he was beginning to tire out because she sure was. Maybe she would be lucky and catch a glimpse of him when she reached the crest of the hill, but she was ill prepared for what she saw.

As she stood at the top of the hill catching her breath, she took a moment to enjoy the breathtaking view. *It truly is a beautiful part of the country we live in,* she thought and then her breath caught in her throat at what she saw below her. *How could it be? It's impossible. I killed him. I know I did,* She thought. But there below her was the alien form of Homlin, devouring the hind quarter of a deer he had obviously just killed.

Pat quickly dropped to the ground and knelt behind a fallen tree. She suddenly regretted having given her knife away. As she studied the beast, she noticed subtle differences. For one, the beast appeared smaller than she had remembered. Of course, that could be because she was a good distance away from this one, and it wasn't towering over her trying to kill her. She also noticed the color was different. Homlin's alien form had been a charcoal black, but the one below her was a mottled green and brown. Was that likely due to its ability to change colors to match its surroundings, much like a chameleon?

The alien suddenly glanced up from his meal and raised his head up in the air as though sniffing the breeze. Pat ducked behind the tree and held her breath. Could it detect her scent from this distance? From which direction was the wind blowing? She breathed more easily when she realized the breeze was coming up the hill and not down, but she stayed hidden behind the tree for several seconds before slowly raising her head to take another look.

The beast had evidently had enough to eat, for when she looked again, it had moved away from its prey and was sitting on its haunches cleaning itself. That's when the biggest shock of all occurred. As it sat there licking the blood off of its hands and arms, the beast started transforming, slowly losing its beast-like qualities and taking on the form of a young human... but not just any human; one that Pat instantly recognized as TJ. And at that moment all the progress she felt they had made over the past few months evaporated into thin air. Clearly, TJ had discovered his true self, and it was Pat's job to protect her loved ones from it no matter what it took.

2

AS A NAKED TJ LAY ON the ground apparently recovering from his recent transformation, Pat used the shelter of the fallen tree to hide her exit, crawling over the crest of the hill. When she was on the other side, she stood up and jogged back in the direction she came, using the time to formulate a new plan. Somehow, she had to get TJ away from Allan, Kendra, and Mimi. She had grown fond of the two girls, which is what had prompted her to talk to Mimi's father. While she had been regretting that decision a short time ago, she now knew it had not been a mistake. From the way TJ had reacted to the news from Mimi, it was apparent to Pat that what may have begun as an innocent childhood crush had grown into much more, at least from TJ's perspective.

And then there was the matter of Allan and his inability to see the truth when it came to TJ. Would he come to his senses once she had told him what she'd seen this afternoon? Or would he just believe it was a story she fabricated to further discredit TJ? Unfortunately, she had been so shocked by what she had seen she had not had the presence of mind to take a picture, and without hard evidence, it was unlikely that she'd be able to convince Allan that TJ was no better than Homlin. No, the time for talking was over. It was time to take action, but what action?

As the log home came into view, Pat had the beginnings of a plan on how to get TJ away from her loved ones. In the last few weeks since his birthday party, TJ had asked more than once if he could go with her on one of her trips to Charlotte. Both Allan and she had put him off each time, telling him that they would need to think it over. It wouldn't be too difficult to persuade Allan to let TJ go with her when she returned to Charlotte in a day or two. She would tell him that it would make for a good home-school field trip, as well as an opportunity for the two of them to bond.

And what do I do with him once I get him away from here, Pat wondered? Unfortunately, at the moment no satisfactory answer came to her. *That's okay,* she told herself. *It won't be the first time I've had to wing it and make it up as I go.* She would just have to trust the answer would come in due course.

3

TJ LAY ON THE LEAF covered ground of the forest, confused and disoriented. What had happened to him? He vaguely remembered being angry. Perhaps angrier than he had ever been before, but over what? He slowly sat up and after his head stopped spinning, looked around. His eyes locked on the carcass of the dead, partially mutilated deer. Had he done that? The answer came almost immediately – yes, he had. He remembered running down the deer as though it had been moving in slow motion, then leaping onto the deer's back and, with one quick twisting movement, snapping the deer's neck. Even as the deer collapsed to the ground already dead, he had leaped onto its haunches to take a large bite. He could still taste the fresh raw meat and could feel the blood around his mouth beginning to clot.

He reached up with one bloody hand and wiped his mouth. The hand came away even bloodier than before, but something was wrong here. Something didn't make sense. He had always been in control of his shapeshifting, but not this time. It was as if this time the transformation had taken him over. He didn't like the feeling of having lost control. Didn't like it at all.

He continued to sit there for a couple more minutes getting his bearings. It was getting late, and he could already feel the air cooling as the sun set. It was only then that he realized he was naked. Damn. *Where the hell are my clothes?* Hopefully, he'd be able to find them between here and home. Otherwise, he'd have a lot of explaining to do. He wasn't all that concerned about finding his way home. He had discovered during other jaunts through the woods that he had a very keen sense of direction. Besides, these woods were like a second home to him; maybe even a first. He often felt more at peace here than in the log cabin.

He began walking up the hill from the direction he'd come, but as he did so, his senses alerted him to a new problem. Over the past month or two, he'd noticed his five senses seemed to be improving. This was especially true when he was in either the canine form or that of the great owl, but even afterward when he returned to human form, the improved senses continued. Now, it was the heightened sense of smell that alerted him to the new danger as he picked up the scent of another human; one he easily recognized as Pat. It was a combination of her perfume and the unique makeup of her own body odor. And it was fresh.

The realization sent a chill through his body unrelated to the falling temperature. Pat had been here just a few dozen yards from where he'd killed the deer. She'd seen him at his worst. Since his birthday party she'd been pretty cool; not nearly as hard to get along with, but this...this could wreck everything. What if she told his dad what she'd seen? Worse yet, what if she told Kendra...or worst of all, Mimi?

No, she might tell Allan, but she wouldn't want Kendra or Mimi to know, would she? It would just complicate her life more. One thing TJ knew about Pat was she didn't like adding complications to her life. He felt sure that was what he'd become to her—a complication.

As he continued walking home, his thoughts about Pat were mixed with thoughts about what had him fleeing to the woods in the first place. As he remembered Mimi telling him that she would be unable to continue home-schooling him, he could feel the anger mounting once again.

Whoa there, boy. Don't go there. Not again. He stopped walking, closed his eyes and took several slow, deep breaths until once again he felt in control. Not that he was any happier about the news, but he realized turning into a blood-thirsty killing machine was not the answer. He'd read enough and seen enough movies to know that he had been jilted, even though he doubted Mimi had re-alized how much her news would hurt him. Not that it made it hurt any less. Maybe it did. At any rate, he would have to get over it. Maybe not immediately, but eventually.

Ahh... wasn't that a pair of blue jeans up ahead and just a little bit beyond that his shirt? See, things were already looking up, but as he started putting his clothes back on, his thoughts continued to swirl, first to Mimi, then to Pat, then back to Mimi again. Talk about complications. His life was becoming way too hard to figure out, but how could he simplify matters? That was a question he couldn't yet answer.

Stormy Family

The next few hours were excruciating for Pat, who tried to act as though nothing was wrong while realizing what she'd seen had dramatically altered her world. Now life was even more complicated than before. By the time Allan had returned home from the hospital, Mimi had left, and TJ had returned home, refusing to talk. Instead, he locked himself in his room, leaving it up to Kendra and Pat to explain the situation to Allan.

"I'm sorry to hear that Mimi won't be able to continue helping with the homeschooling," Allan said, "but maybe it's best in the long run. Maybe I should go talk to TJ."

"I would just let him be for now," Pat advised. "There's really nothing that you nor I can say that will make him feel any better. Time is often the best healer of a broken heart."

"That sounds like somebody speaking from personal experience," Allan said, smiling.

"You could say that," Pat replied. She was thankful when Allan decided to follow her advice and leave TJ alone. The less she had to be around him the easier it would be for her to pretend that everything was still okay between them; at least until Kendra left and she could talk privately with Allan. Unfortunately, Allan seemed to want Kendra to stay around longer than usual and invited her to stay for dinner, which she did. So, it wasn't until later in the evening when Donna had come by to pick up Kendra and her bike so she wouldn't have to ride home in the dark that she and Allan were finally alone.

Meanwhile, TJ had remained in his room, refusing to come out or talk. Allan left a tray of food outside his door, which remained untouched. Pat finally picked it up and took it back to the kitchen where Allan was finishing up the dinner dishes.

Okay, Pat thought; confession time but how to start the conversation?

"What did you mean earlier tonight when you said it might be the best thing if Mimi didn't continue to come over?"

Allan finished drying his hands on a towel before turning in her direction. "I don't know. It just seemed to me that TJ's crush wasn't going away. If anything, he seemed to be developing stronger feelings for Mimi, and I was uncomfortable about it."

"I see," Pat replied with a sigh of relief. "I thought the same thing. That's why I felt compelled to intervene."

Allan stared at her, a confused look on his face. "What does that mean? You felt like you had to intervene? What did you do?"

"I went and talked to Mimi's uncle and father." There, it was out, and it felt good to have admitted it...at least for a moment.

"You what? Without talking to me about it first?" Allan asked incredulously.

"You've been so busy lately that it never seemed a good time to discuss it. Besides, you just said..."

"I know what I said, but that doesn't give you the right to go blabbing about TJ all over town."

"I didn't blab about him all over town," Pat replied, feeling her hackles begin to rise. "I spoke to two people about their daughter and niece, and I didn't mention any specifics when it came to TJ. I'm not an idiot, you know."

"Sometimes I wonder," Allan shot back.

"Well, I'm not. I was very careful to not share anything about the younger boy that had a crush on Mimi. Only that you and I were uncomfortable about it continuing so I thought it would be best if Mimi didn't come around for a while. I never said a word about TJ or his 'differences' that made us uncomfortable, but that does bring me to another point we need to discuss."

"What's that?" Allan asked in a calmer voice.

"You may want to sit down first," Pat said, pointing to the kitchen table.

"That doesn't make me feel any better," Allan replied, but then followed her over and sat down in his customary chair.

"I saw something out there today that I knew you wouldn't want Kendra to know about, but that you need to be aware of."

"O...kay," Allan said slowly.

Pat took a deep breath. She'd been practicing how to tell Allan what she'd seen out on that hillside all evening, but now that it was time, she didn't know what to say. *Maybe I should just keep it to myself,* she thought, but she knew that would be the coward's way out, and she wasn't a coward.

"While I was out in the woods this afternoon looking for TJ, I came upon a deer that had just been killed. Its killer was in the process of eating it." She paused for a moment, trying to figure out how to break the news to him.

"That sounds pretty gruesome," Allan said, "but I'm sure you've seen worse. What kind of animal was it? A mountain lion?"

"No. It wasn't an animal, at least not one of this Earth. It was an alien. In fact, it looked almost identical to Homlin in its alien form."

"Oh, no," Allan said. "There's another one out there? I guess we knew that was at least a possibility."

"It was TJ," Pat said. "I watched him transform back to his human form before I snuck away."

The shocked, hurt look on Allan's face was almost too much to bear. Pat reached out to take his hand, but he pulled away, shaking his head. He stood up and walked over to the sink and stared out the window into the blackness of night.

Maybe I shouldn't have told him, Pat thought. *Maybe it would have been better to keep it to myself.* But he needed to know. He needed to face the truth about TJ. And while this was brutal news, it might just be what was necessary for him to finally open his eyes.

Allan continued to stare out the window, slowly shaking his head. Finally, he turned back around and stared at Pat still sitting at the table.

"And all this time I thought you and TJ had finally worked things out, but clearly you haven't. How long have you been cooking up this story?"

"What are you talking about?" Pat asked, perplexed by the question. "It's what I saw, just this afternoon." Then realizing what he was inferring, her temper flared. "If you think I made this up just to upset you, then you really don't know who I am. You've been living in a fantasy world for so long, you can't tell the difference between what's real and what's not. I'm real, Allan. I'm a real human being who loves you. That...that thing in the other room...it's not human. It's not your son, and honestly, I'm not sure it even can love."

"So is that how you really feel?" Allan asked, beginning to match Pat's anger.

Already regretting losing her temper, Pat didn't know how to answer him. "I don't know. Maybe...sometimes. I mean, this is hard, really hard. It's hard for all of us. I know what it's been like for the past few weeks, and it's been good. It had started to feel like we were a family, but..." The image she'd seen in the woods flashed before her, and she shuddered. How could she ever look at TJ again as part of her family with that image forever emblazoned on her mind?

Over the last few hours, a plan had started to slowly hatch in her mind. She had to get TJ away from Allan. Maybe, with a little time of separation, Allan would come to his senses. And even if he didn't, at least TJ would be out of their life. As ghastly as it was to admit it, she'd even toyed with the idea of killing the boy. She might have been able to follow through with that idea earlier, before TJ's birthday, back in the days when she only thought of him as a dangerous alien—as a foreign thing that threatened Allan and those she loved, but now? She was pretty sure she could do that only under the worse of circumstances. So she had moved on to her original idea, which she'd initiate later tonight. She hoped her outburst of anger hadn't already nixed that option.

"Listen, Allan. I didn't mean what I just said. I'm sorry, but it's been a very trying day," she said trying to mend the rip in their relationship before it grew any larger. "I know you care very deeply for TJ. Over these last few weeks, I have grown fond of him as well."

"You two seemed to be doing better lately," Allan conceded. "I think if you'd just give him a chance, get to know him a little better, I think you'd be able to see what Kendra and I see in him."

There it was; the opening she'd been looking for. "Maybe you're right," she said. *Easy does it*, she thought. *You've got a strong nibble on the line. Don't blow it. Nice and easy.* "What did you have in mind?"

"I don't know exactly," Allan replied. "Spend more time with him. I bet with a little effort you'd find some common interests. Something the two of you could build upon."

Pat nodded. "Yeah, maybe. I'd be willing to give it a try."

She waited, hoping that Allan would come up with the next part on his own. When he didn't respond, she took a gamble and made the suggestion. "How about this idea? What if I took TJ with me to Charlotte tomorrow. We'd have time during the drive to reconnect, and I could show him around the Queen City. He's never been outside this house and the surrounding woods. I bet we'll find plenty of common interests on such a field trip. Just a thought. What do you think?"

"Now you're talking," Allan replied, a smile beginning to form on his face. He walked back to the table and sat down across from her. "It would need to be a short trip. I don't want to overwhelm him his first time away from home."

"Sure, that makes sense," Pat replied as she slowly reeled in the fish named Allan. "I'll just swing by the office for a few minutes. Make sure everything is going all right there, and then after a little sightseeing, we'll head on back. At some point, he needs to learn how to make it in the world. This will be a step in that direction."

Allan nodded as he finally reached out and took Pat's hand. "I do appreciate your making an effort. I just want you two to get along. Maybe I should go let him know what we've decided."

"I'd wait," Pat replied. "It's late, and we've all had a busy day. Let it be a surprise."

"Yeah, you're right. I'm sure TJ will be feeling better after a good night sleep." Allan yawned. "I know I'm looking forward to one. How about you? Ready to turn in?"

"Almost," Pat said. "I just need to make a call or two. I'd like to let my office manager know I'll be bringing a guest so she can be sure the office is clean. You go ahead. I'll join you in a few minutes."

Allan stood up, bending over to give her a kiss; one that lasted longer than his typical goodnight kisses. It only served to make Pat feel even more like a heel for deceiving him. *It's for his own good,* she thought. *Yeah, just keep telling yourself that. You might start believing it.*

She waited until she was sure Allan had made it to their bedroom at the other end of the house. She then took her cell phone out, praying she still had the number in it that she needed. She did. She stared at the contact info for a minute, considering what she was about to do. Finally, she punched the call button.

It took several seconds for the connection to be made. When someone finally did answer, it was with a gravelly voice with a mixture of irritation and sleepiness.

"Hello. This had better be good."

Oops, Pat thought. She had forgotten how early her old friend went to sleep. Oh well, he'd get over it. *It's not like this is the first time I've woken him up.*

"Hello, Oliver. This is Pat. Did I wake you up?"

"Pat? What the hell are you calling me this time of night for?"

"Good to talk to you too," Pat answered, smiling at his reaction. "I have someone I want you to meet, and believe me when I tell you, it's someone you're going to want to meet. Can you meet me at my Charlotte office tomorrow afternoon?"

Pat's Call

1

TJ lay on his bed, still fuming over how the day had gone. It had been nothing but a bad news day all around. First, the news that Mimi would not be able to continue working with him as one of his homeschool teachers. That was bad; very bad. But maybe even worse had been the episode out in the woods where he'd lost all control and had turned into a monstrous form that had him questioning his true identity. And as if that hadn't been bad enough, Pat had seen it happen just when it looked like they might be able to get along as a family.

He heard someone outside his door and a few moments later could smell a mixture of odors. No doubt someone had left a tray of food on the other side of the door, but after his afternoon feeding on the deer, he had no appetite. In fact, for some reason the smell of regular food made him feel a little nauseous. Maybe it was due to his heightened senses. Normally, he doubted he would have been able to detect the food odors, but now they were almost overpowering.

He lay there for quite a while trying to decide what to do next. He couldn't stay locked away in his room forever. At some point, he'd have to go out and face the music; just not tonight. *Please, not tonight. Just let me drift off to sleep. In the morning when I'm rested, maybe I'll have a better idea what to do.* It had been a full day. No doubt about that. Going to sleep sounded like a good idea.

He closed his eyes and was close to drifting off when he heard whispers coming from somewhere outside his room. He'd heard such whispers a few times before when someone was in the kitchen cleaning up after dinner. Evidently, the heating ducts of the two rooms were closely connected, but something was different this time around. Before, he'd been unable to make out more than a few words, and those only because someone had spoken them more loudly. This time each word was crystal clear. He could even make out who said what. It was easy to discern that Pat and Allan were having a pretty heated argument about him.

Nothing particularly new or unusual about that, TJ thought, but he soon changed his mind when Pat confessed to having gone to Mimi's dad and uncle to ask them to keep Mimi away from him.

Why, that bitch! TJ thought as he sat up in bed so he could hear a little better. *She does have it in for me*; a thought that was only further confirmed as he listened to her relate what she had seen out in the woods. *Man, I'm really screwed now.* The one person who had only recently shown some sign of being on his side had seen him at his worst and was now relaying that information to the one person who had continued to stand up for him no matter what.

He was momentarily relieved when he heard Allan defending him and refusing to believe Pat's story, but the relief was short lived when Pat went on to suggest her taking him to Charlotte. On the one hand, the idea of traveling to a big city like Charlotte sounded interesting, but not with Pat. He didn't know what she had up her sleeve, but it couldn't be good.

He was beginning to doze off shortly after Allan had retired, but then Pat made her call. *Who the hell is Oliver and why does Pat want him to meet me?* While he didn't have the answer to either question, one thing was sure. He had no interest in cooperating with Pat's plan. None whatsoever. In fact, he felt it important to get the hell away from her for awhile. She had been right about one thing. It was time for him to broaden his horizons.

2

TJ GLANCED AT THE CLOCK on his nightstand. 12:15 a.m. He'd have several hours to plan his escape while Pat and Allan slept. Suddenly, the idea of eating seemed more appealing, so he quietly opened his door and brought the tray of cold food into his bedroom. He quickly devoured the roast beef sandwich and chips, washing it down with the glass of iced tea. That along with the earlier meal he'd had while in the woods would hold him until he was well away from here.

Next, he had to decide where to go, what to pack, and how to get to his destination. Even as he asked himself the question, the answer came to him.

He ruled out Charlotte. It was too far away for his liking, and besides, it was Pat's territory. If she figured out that he'd gone there, she'd have the advantage in finding him with all her many business connections there. However, over the last few weeks, he'd heard Mimi and Kendra talking about Asheville. He'd even taken the time to research it on the internet. It would do nicely. It was a large enough city that he should be able to get lost in it while also being closer to home, being only about thirty miles from Waynesboro. Having decided his destination, the rest of the plan started to fall into place. He'd have to travel light, with just the basics. That would mean he'd have to have a way to add to his inventory once he was at his final destination. That would require money. After all, money was light and could easily be converted into whatever he needed, like food and warm clothing, which would be important as winter was only a few weeks away.

But where to get the money? Simple enough. He'd borrow it from Allan's cookie jar. He'd watched Allan on numerous occasions return home and empty out his pockets of loose change, which often included taking a few bills from his money clip and dropping it into the cookie jar along with the change. TJ had never seen him empty the jar out, so there must be plenty of money still in it.

TJ unlocked his door again and opened it a crack, listening for any sounds that would let him know if Pat or Allan were still up and moving around. When all he heard was the dull thrum of the heating system, he crept out of his room and down the hall to the kitchen. The cookie jar was on the counter next to the fridge. He opened it to discover it about two-thirds full with cash. He ignored the coins and went straight to the bills. He counted it up and arranged it into a neat stack. The total came to a hundred and twenty-seven dollars. Not a bad nest egg to get this expedition started.

He took a sheet of paper from the notepad stuck on the refrigerator door and wrote the amount on it. Under it he wrote:

$127

I promise to pay you back someday.

Your son, TJ

This makes it a loan, not a theft, TJ told himself as he started back to his room with the money in his hand. He now needed to pack what he'd be taking with him, so he redirected his steps to the storage closet. He dug around until he found Allan's bright blue ski jacket with the rabbit foot attached to the zipper and backpack he occasionally used when going on longer hiking trips. The coat was a couple of sizes too large for him, but at the rate he was growing, it shouldn't take him long to grow into it. Besides, he could use all the luck he could find, so he was happy to take the rabbit foot along with him. He took his treasure back to his room to finish packing.

During all this, he'd continued to consider the other question—how best to travel. He'd read on the internet about people hitchhiking from place to place, but many of those stories didn't have good endings. Hitchhiking was dangerous, and it might make it too easy for Allan or Pat to find him if they figured out the direction he was traveling.

No, he'd take a different means of travel. At first, he considered shifting into the great gray owl form, but while he liked the speed with which he could make his way to Asheville, he couldn't figure out how to carry the supplies he would need once he arrived. But he had already borrowed Allan's backpack a few times while no one was around, and had practiced wearing it as he changed from his human form to his dog and wolf forms. He had confirmed that the backpack still fit well enough for him to wear it in the either of the animal forms. He knew from experience that the wolf form allowed him to travel faster and for longer distances. Of course, he would need to stay out of sight of other humans as much as possible. A backpack carrying wolf would not only draw more attention than he'd want, but it might also lead to him getting shot. At the same time, he could make much better time and could cover a much greater distance in his wolf form than as a human.

He'd just be sure to pack a couple of changes of clothes, along with the ski jacket and a few nutritional bars to tide him over. As he was packing, he came across three other items to take with him. The first one was his most recent copy of the *Mercenaries* computer game. He decided the PlayStation 2 was too heavy and took up too much room, but maybe he'd find somewhere in Asheville he could play the game. Besides, he wanted to take something that Kendra had given him that would help him remember her by. The second item was his copy of Mimi's book. By now the homemade book was dog-eared from being read so many times, but again, it felt important to have something that she had made for him.

It took him a little longer to decide whether to take the third item or not. He finally decided it was just too valuable to leave behind so he tossed the knife and leather sheath Pat had given him into the top of the backpack, then lifted it up to get an idea how much it weighed. He estimated it might be as much as twenty-five or thirty pounds. Not lightweight, but certainly manageable, especially in his wolf form.

He glanced at the alarm clock again. A few minutes before two a.m. He could still get a couple of hours of sleep before heading out well before dawn. He set the clock for four a.m. before turning out the lights and crawling into bed. Tomorrow would be a big day for him. His first time out into the world that he'd merely read about and watched videos of through the internet. Despite the excitement of what awaited him, he managed to fall asleep after only a few minutes.

Thanks

1

TJ's inner clock woke him a few minutes before four a.m., so he leaned over and turned off the clock before it had a chance to go off. Although he was tempted to roll over and go back to sleep, he knew the danger of falling into a deep sleep and awakening much later when the sun had already arisen was too great, so he sat up in bed and stretched.

Was he really going to do this thing? Run away from home to a city he'd never been to, but had only read about on the internet? *Damn right,* he answered his own question, as he kicked the covers off and leaped out of bed. Time to get to it. An exciting life of adventure awaited for him.

It didn't take him long to be ready to head out since he already packed the night before. He put on his favorite pair of blue jeans, a long sleeve plaid shirt, his warmest socks and a pair of tennis shoes. He'd left room for these clothes in his backpack, but had decided it was too dangerous to shift into the wolf form here. He'd wait until he was well into the woods.

He placed the note he'd written the night before in the center of his bed where it could be easily found and looked around his room one last time. He'd miss this place. It had been his sanctuary for his entire life, but he was no longer a kid. It was time to grow up and start his own life, whatever that might be.

He put on the ski jacket he'd 'borrowed' from Allan and shouldered the backpack. He tiptoed down the hall, pausing outside Allan's bedroom door for just a moment.

"Thanks for everything, Dad," he whispered, his eyes suddenly watering as the words caught in his throat. *Enough of that,* he thought. *Can't afford to break down like a silly kid.* He adjusted the backpack to his right shoulder and headed to the kitchen where he poured a box of Cheerios into a plastic bag. Just a little something for the road, he thought, as he sealed the bag and crammed it into his pack, then left out the back door.

He'd discovered in his practice time as a wolf that he had an excellent sense of direction, aided in part by his amazing sense of smell. Still, it seemed easiest to follow one of the secondary roads to Asheville. He'd just stay out of sight of the traffic. He calculated he'd easily be able to cover the thirty or so miles to Asheville before the end of the day, even allowing for a couple of breaks during which he'd shift back into his human form. No way was he going to forget his true form again. The memory of that time still sent a shiver up and down his spine. He waited until he was well out of sight of the house before stopping to make the shift to wolf form. He quickly undressed, stuffing the clothes into the pack, then putting it back on. Now came the tricky part. Shifting to the wolf form while wearing the pack, but he'd practiced this a number of times, so it went smoothly. It even felt like the pack became lighter although he knew it was his strength that had increased. His thick coat would not only keep him warm but would serve to minimize the chafing from the straps.

As he headed in the direction of the highway, the sun peaked above the horizon. Yes, it's going to be a great day for a walk through the woods and a start to a new life.

2

PAT LAY IN BED NEXT to Allan, watching the night slowly turn to day, and remembering the argument from the night before. After making the call to Oliver, she had retired to the bedroom to find Allan still awake. It became clear pretty quickly that he was interested in some makeup sex, and normally Pat would have gone along with it. After all, in times past when they had argued, the makeup sex had been some of the best ever, but not this night. She felt like she had already manipulated Allan too much as it were. To then make love with him seemed too low down, even for her.

Maybe I should call the whole thing off, she thought, as she lay there watching Allan breathing. Call Oliver and cancel the meeting, at least until she was more certain that it was the right thing to do. Even as she considered her different options, she knew she'd not make that call. This was the best option she could take. Time to move ahead.

She climbed out of bed slowly so as not to wake Allan, put on her robe, and walked out to the kitchen to fix coffee. As she did so, she decided a good breakfast was in order. She started preparing French toast, which was Allan and TJ's favorite. *Still trying to get on their good sides,* she thought as she beat the eggs and milk together. *Yeah, maybe, so what?* Of course, it didn't matter how many favorite meals she was willing to fix. None of it would come close to making up for what she was about to do.

Before going further with the breakfast preparation, she fixed two cups of coffee and took one to Allan.

"Wake up, Sleepy Head," she said as she set the coffee on the table next to his side of the bed. "Breakfast will be ready in less than ten minutes."

Allan rolled over and opened his eyes. "What's this? Coffee in bed and breakfast on the way? What have I done to deserve such kind treatment?"

It's not what you've done but what I'm about to do, Pat thought, but instead, she said, "Oh, nothing in particular. Just trying to make up for the terrible things I said last night."

"Thanks," Allan replied as he threw his legs out of bed and reached for the coffee, taking a sip before adding, "Not necessary, but appreciated anyway. What are we having for breakfast? Pop tarts?"

"Hardly," Pat replied, laughing. It was one of the 'breakfasts' she often fixed when they were both in a hurry, but not today. "That is unless you'd prefer them over French toast."

"Hardly," Allan replied. "French toast sounds great. Is TJ up yet?"

"No, I don't think so. I'm on my way to knock on his door now. Hopefully, a good night's sleep and the promise of French toast will coax him out of his lair." Pat realized a second after the words left her mouth how they might sound to Allan. "Sorry, I didn't mean how that sounded."

Allan stood up and walked over to hug her. "Relax, no offense taken. He does sometimes use his room like a lair. We all do."

The two of them stood there hugging for a few more seconds before Allan excused himself and Pat left to awaken TJ. She was surprised to find his bedroom door, which had been closed and locked the night before, was now cracked open. Maybe the smell of coffee had alerted him to breakfast being prepared. She stuck her head through the crack in the door to say good morning, but was surprised to find the room vacant with the bed already made, almost as though no one had slept in it the night before, but what was that on the pillow?

Pat walked over and picked up the folded sheet of paper with Allan's name written on the front. As Pat stared at the note in her hand, a bad feeling took shape just below her solar plexus. *I don't think I'm going to like what this note has to say,* she thought. She slowly unfolded the note:

Dear Dad,

I need some time to sort things out. Don't worry about me. I won't do anything rash. I'll be in touch.

Love,

Your son, TJ

Pat stared at the note for over a minute, reading it several times, trying to discern any possible clues about where TJ had gone. She read how TJ had signed the note over and over.

Your son, TJ...Your son, TJ...Your son, TJ...

She was still trying to decipher its meaning when she heard Allan call from the kitchen.

"Hey, everyone! Let's have some breakfast."

But his words didn't come from behind her where the bedroom door was, but from in front of her.

"I'm one hungry guy this morning," Allan continued.

Pat glanced up in the direction of the sound to the air vent over TJ's bed. The pain in her chest grew as a hand of fear gripped her heart.

TJ had heard their entire conversation. He'd listened to her confession and now knew she was the one that had caused Mimi's expulsion. He also knew she'd spied on him out in the woods. What else had she said while in the kitchen? Of course. He'd also heard her suggestion to take him to Charlotte as a way to work through their issues. That would have been okay except for one thing. She had still been in the kitchen when she'd placed the call to Oliver.

No wonder TJ had decided to run away. She probably would have done the same thing in his place, but how in the hell was she going to explain this to Allan? She was still trying to answer that question when she heard Allan walk into the room behind her.

"What's up? Where's TJ?" Allan asked.

Pat swung around to face him, the open note still in her hand. She opened her mouth to answer him, but nothing came out. She handed the note to him to read.

Hickory

James disconnected the call and placed the cellphone back in the desk drawer. He tried to check for messages daily but had been unusually busy with his heating, and air conditioning business so had missed a couple of days.

The voicemail he heard, though cryptic, was unmistakable. Hickory, a mercenary named after the small North Carolina town where he was born, had been killed. James wasn't surprised by the news. The two of them had been on a couple of different assignments together, and James considered Hickory to be a bit of a loose cannon, always pushing the envelope too far and taking unnecessary risks.

That's why James made it one of his firm policies to know as much as possible about the other members of whatever team he was asked to join. He didn't like putting his life in the hands of unpredictable people like Hickory. After all, he had two young girls who depended upon him to return to them in more or less one piece...and alive.

It was after a particularly harrowing mission that involved two such loose cannons that James began to formulate the idea to regain control over this aspect of his life. Hickory had brought along a younger kid from his hometown who "showed a lot of promise" according to Hickory, though James suspected the kid had bribed Hickory to let him come along. It had almost cost the entire team their lives and would have if James hadn't stepped in.

Never again, he vowed upon returning and hugging his daughters particularly long. He didn't know how, but he needed to find a way to bring some semblance of control back to the mercenary game. He'd grown fond of the extra money. He'd finally been able to pay off the past-due medical bills, but then there was the expense of raising two girls, one of which already needed braces and both who would eventually want to go to college. No, the money was too good, not to mention the thrill, within reason, of the missions. The thrill of well-designed assignments kept him feeling alive, but not when they stepped over the line into near suicide missions.

He was reminded of one of his mother's favorite sayings: where there's a will there's a way. *Well, I have the will so I'll just need to find the way*, James thought as he reached deeper into the desk drawer and pulled out a small black book. He leafed through the pages until he came to the one he'd been looking for with Hickory's name at the top. He tore it out and burned it.

Shack

1

Pat and Allan sat around the kitchen table with their mugs of coffee and TJ's note between them; the breakfast of French toast long forgotten.

"I knew he was upset about Mimi not being able to come over any longer, but I had no idea he would react in this way."

"We have to remember he's a teenage boy who thinks he's in love," Pat replied. "Who knows? Maybe he is in love. That's really not for us to say, but if we can get into the mind of a teenage boy I don't think running away is that unusual." She knew there was a lot more going on with TJ than just his upset over Mimi, but there was really no way she could let Allan know. She had already texted Oliver and canceled their appointment. Now she had to figure out what she could do to help Allan get TJ back. Or did she? Maybe this was a blessing in disguise. What if TJ just disappeared, never to be seen or heard from again? It sure would make her life easier, and maybe, just maybe Allan and she could get on with their lives minus the complication of a son who was really an alien.

As she stared into her half-empty mug of coffee, she considered it. Could she live with herself, knowing that she'd been the cause of his running away? What if they learned later that something terrible had happened to him? What if he was killed, or mugged, or arrested for vagrancy? As callous as it sounded and made her feel, it was this last possibility that concerned her the most. TJ was like a walking time bomb, set to go off at some random time that no one knew. One thing was sure. When he did go off, all hell would break loose. She could see the headlines now:

Alien Discovered Masquerading as Human

The story would go on to describe how a small town veterinarian with assistance from a prominent P.I. from Charlotte had been instrumental in protecting the alien from being discovered.

No. She wanted TJ out of her life, but this wasn't the way. Not to mention that if she was honest with herself, despite everything, she still cared for the boy, alien or not. She thought on one of her father's favorite lessons. Her father, who occasionally admitted to having Buddhist leanings, often quoted Buddhist teaching that the middle way was best. Over the years Pat had learned that there was much wisdom in that approach to life. So, what would be a middle of the road solution for the TJ problem? She didn't have an answer to that question; not yet, but at least it felt like the right question to be asking. That was often the start to finding a solution. So, the first order of business—find TJ.

2

IT HAD BEEN A FULL twenty-four hours and still not a word from TJ. In the first hour, they'd ruled out calling the police or sheriff department. There was just no way they could take the risk of involving them. Allan had called Kendra and Mimi just to let them know what had happened. Neither of them had a clue where TJ might have run off to but promised to be in touch if they heard from him.

"Let's try not to panic," Pat finally said. "Many kids who run away stay gone less than a day, then they either calm down or get hungry and come on home. Let's give TJ a little time."

Allan reluctantly agreed, but now it was the next morning and still no word from TJ.

Pat and Allan sat around the kitchen table, lost in their own thoughts. Finally, Allan asked for about the tenth time in the last twenty-four hours, "Where do you think he would go? He's never been anywhere other than this house and the land around it... except for that brief excursion to Homlin's place. Do you think he'd try to go back there?"

Pat shook her head. "No, I don't think so, but I could be wrong." An idea suddenly came to her, and she stood up. "I may know how to find out where he went."

"How?" Allan asked.

"Follow me," Pat replied as she walked into Allan's office and sat down in front of the computer. "TJ has spent countless hours in front of this thing. It's become his window to the world in many ways. Let's just see what's in its browser history."

Pat pulled up the list of sites visited over the last month. There were hundreds of different pages ranging from gaming websites, mostly related to a game called *Mercenaries*, to sites about wolves, owls, and several other animals. Pat scrolled down, scanning through the list like a speed reader and then suddenly stopped.

"There, that's where he has headed," she said as she pointed to the screen and a long list of sites all with the word, Asheville NC, in their name.

"Asheville?" Allan asked. "Why Asheville?"

"Why not Asheville?" Pat replied. "It makes sense to me. It's reasonably close and a fairly good size city. Should be fairly easy to stay incognito there."

"Yeah, I guess that makes sense," Allan replied. "So, now what? Do we drive over and see if we can find him?"

"No," Pat replied. "Least not yet. TJ is too smart just to be standing on a street corner waiting for us to find him, and Asheville is too large, but I know someone who may be able to help. His name is Shack Lawson. He's a P.I. in Asheville of some dubious reputation, but he and I have always gotten along pretty well." She decided it best not to mention the number of times Shack had tried unsuccessfully to get her into bed. "I'll call him later today."

Allan glanced at his watch. "It's already 9:30. Why not call him now?"

Pat chuckled. "Shack doesn't have much use for early morning calls, and believe it or not, 9:30 is still way too early. I'll give him a call around noon. I'll probably still be waking him up, but at least he won't be so ornery then. You go on to work. You've got lives to save."

"Yeah, and cats to spay," Allan agreed. "Keep me posted though."

"Sure thing," Pat said as she stood up and kissed him. "I know how important TJ is to you," *and I'm discovering how important he is to me as well,* she thought, surprised by her own admission.

3

TJ'S LEISURE JOURNEY to Asheville took him along the Blue Ridge Parkway to Craven Gap where he found himself in the late afternoon. Off in the westerly direction, the sunset turned the clear sky a brilliant mixture of orange and red clouds against a deep blue sky while down below in the valley set the skyline of Asheville, the lights beginning to twinkle in preparation for another late fall evening.

TJ had shifted back to human form for the last few miles, not wanting to take the chance of running into other humans along the road as a wolf. He stood now in awe of the scene below him. He had known that Asheville was one of the fastest growing areas of western North Carolina, but none of the pictures he'd seen of it on the internet had come close to capturing its beauty or its size.

I think I'm going to like it here, he thought, as he studied the skyline that included several large buildings highlighted with a line of purplish mountain ranges in the background. He'd searched on the internet for cheap places to stay but hadn't found anything under fifty dollars a night. At that rate, his borrowed nest egg would be gone in no time, but his luck was holding for the night temperatures promised to be unseasonably warm. He figured he'd just sleep in one of Asheville's many parks, at least until he found a job.

He'd start his search for gainful employment first thing the next day. Tonight, he'd treat himself to a good meal in a restaurant close to the park he'd selected for his temporary housing. If he was careful, his stash should easily last until his first paycheck. He might even drop in on one or two of the nightspots of which he'd read. The Orange Peel, a favorite bar and entertainment venue that had been open for three years, had already become well known for some of the popular bands they'd hosted. Yes, his new life in Asheville was going to be very good.

Asheville

1

As TJ entered the main business section of Asheville, the sun set behind the western range of mountains and soon the day turned to night. He stopped a couple of people on the street and asked where a good place to eat could be found. Two out of the three recommended the Mellow Mushroom, and the last one even gave him directions to it.

He was less than a block away and could see the sign up ahead when his keen hearing picked up the piercing scream of a woman followed by several loud words of anger off in the distance, accompanied by the equally angry retorts of a man. TJ took a couple more steps towards the restaurant, but then stopped when he heard a second even more blood-curdling scream sounding as though the woman was being killed.

He followed the voices down a narrow side street with poor lighting. Hearing a third scream, he picked up his pace to a run while the few people he saw around him appeared to ignore it all. *Maybe they don't hear it as well as I am*, he thought as he turned down an alleyway and saw a man and woman at the end of the alley grappling with each other. The man threw the woman down and appeared to be trying to wrestle her pocketbook away from her while she held onto it tenaciously.

"Hey, stop that!" TJ yelled as he ran towards them. "Leave her alone."

The man ignored him as he continued to try to yank the purse out of her hand but only ended up dragging her along the ground. As TJ ran towards them, he lifted his pack off his back and prepared to sling it at the large man's head, but when he did the man deftly ducked, and the pack swung through space, throwing TJ off balance.

"Now!" TJ heard the man shout, and with that, the woman was suddenly standing up next to him and slinging her pocketbook at his head. Her aim was considerably better than his had been. It hit him hard against his left side, and he fell, slamming his head on the dirty pavement of the alley.

The next few moments became a blur for TJ, as the man and woman jumped on him and beat him viciously; the man kicked him with his sharp-toed boots while the woman continued to hit him with her purse that felt like it must be filled with bricks. At one point TJ felt himself beginning to shift shape, he couldn't tell which and it didn't matter. He lost consciousness before the shift could take.

2

HE AWOKE SOMETIME LATER with a terrible odor assaulting his nose. He slowly opened his eyes but found himself still in the dark. It took him several minutes before he was conscious enough to realize he was resting on a mound of smelly garbage in an enclosed area designed for such trash. His head felt like the top of his skull might jettison from the rest of his body, and his ribs and groin ached from where the man had kicked him multiple times. He slowly rose from his prone position, only to crack his head against the hard metal top of the dumpster in which he'd been thrown.

After waiting for the stars to clear, he pushed the top open and found he was still in the alleyway. He looked around for his backpack, but his assailants had apparently taken it with them. That's when he noticed he was colder than he'd been before. They'd also taken ownership of his ski jacket. He stuck his right hand into his jean pocket and came away empty. They'd taken all his money as well. He leaned on the side of the dumpster, waiting for vertigo to pass, and felt drops of blood trickle down the side of his head.

"Welcome to Asheville," he whispered as he slowly collapsed back into the pile of garbage.

3

TJ AWOKE THE NEXT MORNING to the sound of a loud and persistent beep, beep. He reached one arm out to hit the snooze button of his alarm clock, but his hand landed on a wet, slimy pile of unknown origin. His eyes flew open at the same time his nose awoke to a strangely familiar stench. He groaned as the memory of the night before flooded into his awareness. *One of the worse nights of my life,* he thought. He vaguely remembered leaving the dumpster at one point during the night only to return less than an hour later. The night temperature had plummeted as a brisk, chilling wind blew through the streets and alleyways of Asheville. He looked for some other shelter from the wind, but every place he looked had already been taken by someone else. It was a harsh welcome to the homeless community. He had read on the internet about the growing population of homeless people in Asheville but hadn't fully comprehended how many men, women and yes, even children lived on the street without a home to go to.

And now I'm one of them, he thought. The realization sent a new chill through his body; one independent of the cold temperatures. Finally, after being yelled and cursed at by several of the homeless, TJ retraced his steps back to the dumpster, which suddenly looked more welcoming than it had when he'd first abandoned it.

I sure hope someone hasn't taken my spot, he thought as he lifted the lid and looked inside, then breathed a sigh of relief when he found it still empty. "Home, sweet home," he whispered as he climbed in and pulled the lid down to reduce the wind. Okay, maybe not sweet, but at least it would serve his purpose for the night. Tomorrow, he'd start pounding the pavement for a job and turn this downward spiral of his life around.

But what the hell was that irritating noise that had awoken him and continued to blast in his ear? As he had the thought, he felt the dumpster suddenly shudder and then shake more violently as it was lifted into the air. He jumped up, hitting his head once again on the hard metal of the dumpster's top, then wincing in pain, pushed the top open. The dumpster started tilting towards the garbage truck that had lifted it into the air.

"Hey! Hold on. I'm inside here!" he shouted at the top of his voice. "Wait just a minute!"

The two sanitation workers who looked like they might have spent their own night in a dumpster stared first at him and then at each other with shocked looks. Finally, one of the men waved at a third man in the truck's cab, and a second later the dumpster stopped moving.

"What the hell you doing in there?" one of the men asked.

"Trying to keep from freezing," TJ replied as he crawled to the edge of the dumpster and jumped down to the alleyway.

"Well, I've never," the other man replied. "Getting so you can't take a step in this town without stepping on some bum."

"Take it easy, Jed," the first man answered back. "If it weren't for this job, that could be you or me."

His comrade grunted something unintelligible as he waved to the truck driver to resume emptying the dumpster.

"Speaking of jobs," TJ said as he turned to the one who had expressed some sympathy for his plight. "Know where I can get one?"

"Nah," the man replied, suddenly appearing far less interested in him. "Especially not looking and smelling like that."

TJ looked down at his stained shirt and pants. His gaze traveled down his body to his tennis shoes, where a dried banana peel stuck to one of them. He kicked it off. The man made a good point. No one would consider hiring him in his current condition.

"Do you know where I can find a bathroom then?"

"You may be able to sneak into the library when it opens at eight. It's just a couple of blocks away," the man replied. "Just don't tell anyone I told you so. And stay clear of their rent-a-cop."

The man climbed onto the side of the truck, and the empty dumpster was lowered to the ground. "You're new to the street, aren't you?"

"Maybe," TJ replied, suddenly wary of answering such a question.

"There's a shelter over on Ravencroft, not far from here. You can ask anyone for directions. I know you might want to go it alone, but if it gets too bad, they should be able to help."

"Thanks, I appreciate the information."

"No sweat, kid. Like I said, there but for the grace of God...." And with that, the truck pulled out onto the main street and away.

TJ followed the truck out of the alley to the main road where the city was slowly starting to awaken. As he walked along following the directions the garbageman had given, he noticed several people glaring at him, and one or two even appeared to cross the street to avoid him. Not that he could blame them. He surely couldn't brag about his appearance and was finding it hard to put up with his own smell.

He found the library just a couple blocks away but continued to walk around until it opened. He needed to pee badly, and the walking seemed to help. As soon as the doors opened, he entered along with several other patrons who frowned at him but refrained from saying anything.

Locating the bathrooms near the rear of the building, he rushed over to the closest urinal and relieved his aching bladder. He then walked over to the line of sinks to clean up. As he stared into the mirror, he gasped. Who was that scruffy, bloodstained kid staring back at him with the matted, greasy hair? He tilted his head to one side to get a better look at the scalp wound. He pulled a couple of paper towels from the dispenser, wet them and tenderly cleaned the wound. It had bled quite a bit but didn't appear to be that deep. As long as it didn't get infected, it would heal within a few days. He used several other wet towels to clean away the blood and dirt before finally clogging one of the sinks with a towel so he could soak his head, using the hand soap to wash his hair.

While he cleaned himself, an elderly man entered the bathroom, paused a moment to glare disapprovingly at him, then quickly relieved himself at the line of urinals before disappearing without bothering to wash his hands. TJ took another handful of towels to dry himself and was in the process of blow drying his hair with the one lone hand dryer when he felt a firm hand grab his shoulder from behind and spun him around.

"What the hell you think you're doing, boy?" A large man with a belly that extended over his belt dressed in a light blue uniform glared down at him. *Ahh, the guy warned me about this rent-a-cop.*

"Just using the facilities," TJ answered, in as light-hearted tone as he could muster.

"These here facilities are for patrons only," the man said as he continued to grip TJ's shoulder painfully hard. "You got yourself a library card or some other form of ID?"

"Gosh, I ran out of the house so fast this morning, I forgot my wallet," TJ replied.

"Yeah, I just bet you did. I should run you in for vagrancy."

"Oh, that won't be necessary," TJ replied as he tried to twist out of the man's grasp. "My mom and I are staying at the shelter over on Ravencroft, so I'll just be heading on over there."

"All right then," the cop replied finally releasing his grip. "Get yourself back over there, and I don't want to see you back around these parts, you hear?"

"Yes, sir," TJ said as he backed away from the man, then quickly turned to exit the bathroom before the cop changed his mind.

Job Hunting

1

Pat held out to 12:30 before calling Shack. As she expected, the phone rang several times without him picking up, so she hung the phone up on the fourth ring before it had time to switch over to voicemail. She called a second time and hung up again after the fourth ring. Shack picked up on the third ring of the third try.

"Who the hell is this, and I swear if you're trying to sell me something I will personally hunt you down and rub you and your family out."

"Good afternoon, Shack. It's Pat Vogt. See you're as pleasant as always."

There was a momentary pause on the other end, then a much more pleasant voice answered. "Well, hello, good looking. To what do I owe this pleasant surprise? Have you finally come to your senses and dumped that no account vet and are ready to accept one of my many invitations to dinner?"

"No to the first, and you know good and well your invitations were never just for dinner," Pat replied smiling. "I'm afraid this isn't personal, but business. I need your expertise in locating a missing person who we're pretty sure is in Asheville."

"Oh," Shack replied, clearly disappointed. "In that case, let me start my billing clock. Okay, go ahead."

"The missing person is a teenage boy. I can send you a recent picture. He left home yesterday morning."

"And who wants to find him?"

"I do...and Allan," Pat replied.

"Your vet boyfriend?" Shack asked, growing more perturbed by the moment. "What's the teenager's name and what's his relationship to this Allan guy?"

"His name is TJ, and his relationship... it's complicated. Let's just say for the record he's Allan's adopted son. Listen, Shack, I called you because I knew you

131

had the connections there in Asheville and that you'd be...discreet in your inquiries. After all, we do go back a ways..." This was Pat's way of reminding Shack of some of the secrets she had on him.

"Yes, no need to bring up the past, sweetheart," Shack replied. "Email me the picture along with anything else that might help me locate him, including anything he might have taken with him. Sometimes, we get lucky and these runaways hock items when they get desperate for money. We might get a lead that way."

"The only thing I can think he might have taken that he could hock would be a knife I gave him as a birthday present that my dad had given to me. I think I may still have a photo of it. If so, I'll send that along as well."

"Good," Shack replied. "I'll get the word out and let you know what I turn up. Of course, there is one other condition for hiring me."

"Forget it. I'm not going to sleep with you."

"That really cuts me to my core. I was simply going to ask you to have dinner with me," Shack replied, then added, "And we'd see where it went from there."

"I'll send the picture of TJ in a few minutes, and if I find the picture of the knife, I'll send it later," Pat replied, then hung up.

2

TJ'S JOB HUNTING PLAN was simple. He walked around the downtown section of Asheville looking for Help Wanted signs. It didn't take long before he found one posted for a restaurant looking for servers and a dishwasher.

Great, TJ thought as he pushed the door open and walked in. The more positions needed, the better his odds. He squared his shoulders and tried standing taller as he watched a young woman with blonde hair in a ponytail stroll through the swinging door, drying her hands with a towel. She wore black slacks and a khaki blouse with a name tag that identified her as Renee.

"We're not open yet," Renee said as her gaze took in all of TJ's appearance, a frown growing on her face.

"I'm here for the job, Miss Renee," TJ said, pointing to the sign in the window.

"Really? Which one?"

"The one that pays the most," TJ replied smiling his most engaging smile.

"How old are you anyway?" Renee returned his smile then tried to hide it with her hand.

"How old do I need to be?"

"Eighteen for the dishwashing job, twenty-one for the waiter position because we serve alcohol."

"I guess I better go for the dishwasher job then," TJ replied.

"Really? You're eighteen?" the woman asked, cocking her head to one side. "Let me see your driver's license."

"Sorry, I don't have one," TJ replied. "I know I look young for my age, but why should my looks or age matter if I can do a good job washing dishes?"

"Because that's the law," she replied. "And if I were to hire you and it turned out you weren't the legal age to work, I could lose my job, and that's not going to happen. I have a three-year-old who has this habit she can't seem to kick of eating three meals a day. Now, please leave. You're smelling up the place."

And that brief job interview was the closest he came all day in becoming gainfully employed, despite inquiring at almost a dozen different businesses. By the time night fell for the second time since his arrival in Asheville, TJ felt dejected, tired and hungry as hell. *Maybe I should check out the shelter over on Ravencroft*, he thought, but it felt too much like he'd be admitting defeat, and he wasn't ready to throw in the towel.

With the sun setting in the west, the temperature started dropping again. It felt like he was in store for another cold night, which probably meant another night of sleeping in the dumpster; this time on an even emptier stomach than the night before. As he took a shortcut through Pack Square Park, he noticed an old lady with a small child feeding the pigeons, the birds flocking around the two of them. A thought suddenly came to him.

He might end up sleeping in a dumpster again tonight, but no way was he going to bed hungry. He had ways to feed himself not available to other homeless people. He walked around the park looking for a secluded area where he could initiate his plan without being discovered. He found a corner of the park where the lights had apparently burned out and not been replaced. Perfect for his night escapade, he thought as he slipped behind a row of shrubbery. He quickly undressed, carefully folding his smelly shirt and pants on top of each other, then stuffing his socks inside his tennis shoes before placing the shoes on top of the clothes. He then hid the pile deep within the hedge and prayed no one would find them.

He shivered in the cold night temperatures for only a couple of minutes before the shift to the great gray owl form began. Owls were great hunters, used to searching for their prey in the evening, and sighting one in an urban setting wasn't that uncommon. And one thing TJ had noticed during the day, Asheville had an abundant population of gray squirrels and even a few of the albino ones more commonly seen in the Brevard area. He'd heard Mimi talking about her Uncle Bo hunting squirrels and bringing them home to make a stew from them. Squirrel stew hadn't sounded all that appetizing to TJ at the time, but it sure sounded better than eating one raw. Too bad, he berated himself. Beggars can't be choosers, and neither can hungry, homeless kids.

He took his time making the shift. After all, it had been quite a while since he'd turned himself into an owl, and he was afraid he might be out of practice. When the transformation was complete, he stretched first one wing and then the other before using them to fly up onto the limb of a nearby tree. The owl form was the favorite of all his animal forms, and while he had no desire to become stuck in a form again, if he had to choose one to be stuck in, he would choose to be an owl. After all, the ability to fly was such a freeing experience.

It didn't take long to detect his first prey. In owl form, his sight and hearing were even better than the heightened senses he had as a human. He could easily detect the movement of a small mammal on the ground below. He waited for it to move into the clearing below the tree. He then quietly launched himself into the air with a flap of his wings made virtually silent in flight by the special design of his feathers. As he descended on his prey, he identified it as a good size hare just before he fanned out his wings and knocked the rabbit over with his talons, hitting it in the head and neck. He felt the snap of the rabbit's neck and its final death throes underneath him. He looked around to see if anyone was approaching, but his silent assault assisted by the darkness had gone unnoticed.

He dragged the carcass into the bushes not far from where he had stashed his clothes, feeling fortunate that his first hunting spree had gone so well. It also dawned on him that if he could find some matches, he could start a fire and cook his meal, which sounded much more appetizing than eating it raw. He decided to give it a shot. He found his pile of clothes, transformed back into human form and retrieved the rabbit. He then stuffed it into a plastic grocery bag he had found along the pathway leading back to the lit part of the park.

Locating a book of matches took a little longer, but he finally found some that had been left behind on one of the sidewalk cafe tables along with a pack of cigarettes. He took both, figuring he might be able to trade the cigarettes for something later. He had read enough about living out in the wild to know that he needed to dress the rabbit before cooking it. *Sure wish I still had my knife,* he thought. That and the ski jacket were his two greatest losses when it came to practicality, though he also regretted losing Mimi's book and the computer game Kendra had given him.

But practical matters were becoming increasingly important to him, and right now he needed to be able to clean the rabbit carcass so he could cook it. He solved the problem with a soda pop bottle he had found on his way back to the park. Holding the bottle by its neck, he broke it on the concrete curb and came away with a sharp piece that would do nicely for cleaning the rabbit and also as a weapon in case anyone else tried to take advantage of him. Life on the streets might be hard, but it was also a good teacher if you could survive the lessons.

That night he retired to the dumpster with a full stomach of cooked rabbit and a tool and weapon of the glass bottle. He had lined one end of the dumpster with several layers of newspapers he'd accumulated during the day and had sequestered the bags of garbage that had been tossed in it to the other end. He would use the remaining newspapers as a blanket. He might be cold, but he'd be warm enough to make it to the next day. Maybe his luck in finding a job would be better tomorrow, and one thing he also added to his plans. He needed to find a better place to live than the dumpster. After all, it wouldn't be long before it would be filled with garbage again.

Miss Precious

1

By the middle of the next day, TJ had concluded that when it came to getting a job, he was in a no-win situation. Not only was his disheveled appearance a major obstacle, but even worse, he didn't have the necessary identification papers or a note from a parent or guardian. Without such papers, no one was willing to give him the time of day, much less take a chance with him by giving him a job.

I can work. Sure I'm a young kid, but I can still do things like washing dishes, waiting on people, clearing tables, you name it. So why won't someone give me a chance? The answers were all the same. No ID papers, no work, or you're dirty, and you smell, so get out of here, but it wasn't his fault he was dirty and smelled. If he could get a job, he'd be able to get his clothes cleaned and even take a bath somewhere.

He decided he needed to take a break from job hunting. As Kendra had told him more than once, "You might not be able to stop bad things from happening to you, but you are in control of your attitude about those things." Or something like that. He had to admit at the moment his attitude sucked, so he decided to change not only his attitude but also his form. Maybe seeing the city from a different perspective would help.

He returned to the park that was rapidly becoming his second home. It was the closest he could come to his old habit of taking long walks in the woods when he was having a bad day. Plus, there were places in the park where he could shift to an animal form without being seen. He thought about shifting back into the owl form but decided to save it for later when he needed to hunt for his next meal. There had been enough rabbit left over for a good sized breakfast, so he could wait until the evening to hunt. Instead, he decided to explore Asheville in his dog form. He had noticed quite a few people walking around the city with their pet dogs, so maybe he'd get better treatment as a dog than as a human. In either case, he could explore the area freely while covering a good bit of ground as well.

As he made the shift, the first thing he noticed was that he felt warmer in his canine coat than he did as a human with only a shirt and jeans to keep him warm. He also noticed a change in the people around him when he left his hiding place and started walking around the park. As a homeless person, people either ignored him completely or were antagonistic towards him. As a dog, many people continued to ignore him. Those who did notice him tended to be much friendlier and easy-going with him. A few even took the time to pat him on the head or talked to him as he walked by them.

"Where are you going, boy?"

"Lost your owner, big guy?"

"Oh, what a handsome dog you are. Dad, can we take him home with us?"

Of course, there were those who were also intimidated by his large size and would either cross the street to get away from him, or stop and wait for him to pass, but even they didn't treat him harshly.

Funny, TJ thought. *Asheville seems to be friendlier to animals than to homeless people.*

He was enjoying his afternoon romp around the city when he found himself in a new section he'd not yet explored. The houses and buildings were older here and not as well kept, and the smaller park he found appeared to be going to seed and strewn with litter. He was about to turn around and retrace his steps when his canine senses were propelled into high alert by a bark that reminded him of the rabbit squeal he'd heard on the internet. Another dog was in trouble. He trotted towards the sound, his hackles raised.

In the far corner of the park, he found an old playground with a set of swings, slides, and a merry-go-round in dire need of repair. Partially hidden under one of the slides was a small spaniel-looking dog trying to fend off the attack of three younger and larger dogs. The lead dog looked to be a cross between a pit bull and a larger, shaggier dog and was close to TJ's size. His two companions were smaller than the shaggy dog, but both the black and tan shepherd and the black short haired dog looked like they could hold their weight in any fight.

TJ could just make out the greying muzzle of the spaniel sticking out from her improvised shelter as she growled and snapped at her three tormentors. Three big bruisers against one small old girl didn't seem fair at all to TJ, but then he remembered the last time he'd tried to help out a lady in distress. His head was still sore from where she'd laid him out. He started to back away. No need to interfere. It wasn't his fight.

Just at that moment, the three dogs charged the spaniel, and the shepherd grabbed her by the nape of her neck and started pulling her out from under the slide where the other two dogs could get to her as well. Before he realized what he was doing, TJ barked his most fierce and intimidating bark, and he charged into the fracas. He snapped at the hindquarters of the shepherd and was pleased to feel his teeth sink into the muscular rump, followed a second later with a high pierced bark of pain.

The shepherd released its hold on the spaniel, who quickly retreated under the slide. As the shepherd turned to ward off his attacker, TJ took the opportunity to place him between the three assailants and the spaniel. He stood with his front legs wide apart and snarled a warning which he hoped meant something like; *You want a piece of me? Come and get it!* In dog speak. The two smaller dogs backed away, but the pit bull lunged at him, trying for his throat. Fortunately, TJ saw the attack coming and was able to sidestep as he clamped down on his attacker's right ear, ripping a large chunk of it off in his mouth. He promptly spit it out, surprised at the exhilaration he felt from the taste of blood.

The pit bull backed off, shaking his head, sending droplets of blood flying off in all directions. The three dogs stood frozen in a semi-circle facing TJ, but none of them were prepared to further the fight. They slowly backed away and finally trotted out of the park.

TJ stood watching them until he was sure they weren't going to try to counterattack, then turned back to see if the spaniel was okay, but she was no longer under the slide. She'd used his diversion to slip out the back way and was even now hightailing it out of the park in the opposite direction.

I'll be... TJ thought. *What an ungrateful...* but then he stopped himself. Truth be told, if he'd been in her situation, he might have done the same thing. *At least she didn't hit me with her purse.* He chuckled to himself at the thought. He'd done a good deed. That was what mattered, and he had lived to tell about it, even though he didn't have anyone to share it with at the moment.

He glanced down at the ground where the piece of ear laid in the dirt. Was the excitement he'd felt from tasting blood an indication he was becoming too much dog and in jeopardy of losing himself again? He didn't think so, but he was also not interested in finding out. Time to return to where he'd hidden his clothes so he could shift back to his human form, but he'd learned something else important today. He was warmer as a dog with his thick coat than he was as a human with just a shirt and pair of pants. If he got too cold tonight, he'd shift back to dog form at least for a little while.

2

BY THE TIME TJ HAD returned to Pack Square Park, found his clothes and shifted back to his human form, the sun was dipping behind the mountains, and the temperature began to drop again. And he was growing hungry again, having finished off the last of the rabbit earlier in the day. He had noticed several others of the homeless community sitting along the streets of Asheville panhandling for change, but he wasn't quite ready to go that route, although with the temperatures dropping more each day, it wouldn't be long before he'd have to do something to come up with warmer clothes. He was still thinking about what that might be when he saw the old spaniel trotting down the sidewalk in front of him. She appeared to be favoring one of her front legs but otherwise was no worse for wear.

He decided to follow her to see where she went. She took a straight path through the park to the other side where she met up with an old man wearing khaki pants with a cardboard sign propped up beside him that read:

Homeless Vet

Support Your Troops

Beside the sign set a plastic Tupperware container with an American flag sticking out of it along with a few dollar bills. The dog leaped into the old man's lap and licked his gray-bearded face, much to the vet's satisfaction.

"Welcome home, Miss Precious," he said, laughing heartily at her antics. He placed one hand on his head to keep the camouflaged cap from falling off.

But TJ's attention focused on one particular detail that stood out over all the rest. The man was wearing his dad's blue ski jacket, complete with the rabbit foot attached to the zipper. He watched as the man took a morsel of food from his jacket pocket and fed it to the dog. While she munched on it, he gently checked her paw.

"Is she okay?" TJ asked as he approached the two of them, his eyes still focused on the jacket.

"Yeah, she'll be okay," the man replied friendly enough. "Looks like she might have gotten herself into a bit of a scrap while she was away."

"She did," TJ replied. "It was off of Hilliard Avenue in that park. Three dogs were after her." As TJ talked, the spaniel climbed down from her owner's lap and walked over to him. She sniffed at his leg for a second before jumping up on him in a friendly manner.

"She wandered that far away?" the vet asked, then noticing her antics, continued. "That's odd. She never takes to strangers, but she sure has taken to you." He studied TJ for a moment before asking, "Did you help ole Precious out?"

"Let's just say; we've met before and leave it at that."

"Okay," the man said. "Thank you kindly for whatever you might have done." He reached out his right hand. TJ hesitated for a moment before realizing he was offering to shake hands. As he took the man's hand, he noticed he was missing a couple of fingers, and the remaining ones were scarred and arthritic looking with swollen knuckles. "I'm Luke, and this here is Precious."

"I'm TJ. Good to meet the two of you."

"You new to these parts?" Luke asked as he released TJ's hand. "Don't remember seeing you around here before."

"Yeah, been here a few days," TJ answered. "Listen, I hate to bring this up, having just met and all, but well...that jacket you're wearing is mine...well, my dad's, but I borrowed it from him."

"Is it now?" Luke replied noncommittally. "You know what they say about the law around here."

"No, what do they say?"

"Possession is nine-tenths of the law," Luke replied with a chuckle. "If it's your jacket, but you and I have never met, and I'm now wearing it, how could that be?"

"I was mugged and robbed the first night I got here."

"Oh, were you now? Don't tell me you fell for the ole 'damsel in distress scam?'"

"Yeah, I guess so," TJ replied, hanging his head. "But that doesn't make it any less mine."

"No...no it don't," Luke replied, "but my possessing it sure does. Listen, let me ask you something. Where you been staying?"

"Around," TJ replied.

"You're the kid been sleeping in the dumpster off of Spruce Street, ain't you?"

"Maybe," TJ finally admitted.

"Yeah, well you sure smell like it," Luke said with a chuckle. "Listen, I'm not a big fan of slick Saul and Sally's tactics. They're the ones that welcomed you to town, but sky blue is my favorite color so when I saw him wearing this here jacket, I traded for it. So, you want it back; you'll need to trade me for it."

"I don't have anything to trade," TJ replied, upset at how much it sounded like a whine.

"How about you let me be the judge of that," Luke replied. "Now, tell me the truth. Did you help Precious out of her scrap with those three dogs?"

TJ nodded. "Yeah, but I can't tell you how."

"That don't matter," Luke replied as he took off the jacket. "That's good enough for me. There's nothing on this planet more important to me than this here ole dog, and if you saved her from being mauled by three bully dogs, I'd say that's a pretty good trade." He held the jacket out to TJ. "What do you say?"

"Yeah, I guess so," TJ finally agreed as he took the jacket from him. "But what will you wear?"

"Oh, don't worry about me. I still got my old Army coat. It's not a pretty blue like this one, but it's warm, and I think Precious likes it more on me than the blue one, but there's one more thing. You can't take that coat back to that smelly dumpster. You come with Precious and me. We'll find you somewhere to stay."

Hunting

1

Pat didn't hear back from Shack until the next evening.

"I'm betting by the time this is over, it'll be you insisting we have dinner and on your tab," Shack said as his greeting.

"Since when did you start believing in miracles?" Pat retorted. "You got something for me besides pipe dreams?"

"Yeah," Shack replied. "Word is on the street that a new kid showed up a day or two ago. Of course, a new kid on the street is hardly news, but in this case, it was. No one knows where he's from, but rumor has it he's been sleeping in a dumpster off of Market Street. He fits your boy's description."

Pat groaned at the thought of TJ sleeping in a dumpster, realizing it was her fault. "Can you follow up on it, and let me know what you find?"

"Of course, little lady," Shack replied. "Your wish is my command. I also heard of a new steak and seafood restaurant that just opened that's supposed to have a killer wine list. Want me to make reservations?"

Pat didn't bother to answer, but as she hung up the phone, she had a smile on her face.

2

"LOOK, SOME OF MY FRIENDS and I are going to hang out tonight. It's not supposed to be all that cold. We have a place that's pretty safe, and there will be a fire and blankets for when you're ready to crash. You're welcome to come along if you don't already have other plans." Luke tried to keep from smiling as he said that last part.

"Let me check my calendar and see if I can fit something else in," TJ answered, playing along, and a second later he added, "You're in luck. I happen to have tonight free." Then he stopped himself. "Ahh, I don't have anything to contribute, but if you give me a little bit of time, I can maybe come up with a rabbit or two. If not that, how about a squirrel?"

Luke looked at him as though trying to figure out if he was serious. "How you going to get a rabbit or squirrel?" he asked.

"Oh, I've got my ways," TJ answered. "Tell me where the gathering is, and I'll be there. I'll bring what I can."

Luke gave him directions, then stood up and started packing up his belongings, which included a few dollars he'd collected during the day. He started to stick the money in his pant's pocket, then stopped.

"Here, you take this just in case the rabbits and squirrels don't cooperate."

TJ looked at the money Luke held in his gnarled hand. "I can't take your money. You worked hard for it."

"Yeah, right. Sitting on my ass all day looking pathetic is hard work, but I'm used to it," Luke replied still holding out the money. When TJ didn't move to take it, he stepped forward and stuck it into TJ's shirt pocket. "Look, man, if you're going to be on the street, you gotta learn not to let your pride get in the way. You helped out my Precious earlier today without any expectation of getting anything from it. Well, I believe in karma so consider this a little karma back to you."

TJ wasn't sure what his new friend meant by that last comment, but he realized he was in no position to refuse Luke's generosity. "Okay, but that means the fattest rabbit will be yours."

"That's fine. I haven't had a good rabbit stew in ages. Good hunting, boy. Come on, girl," Luke called to Precious. "Let's go round up the others."

The two of them headed off in the opposite direction from TJ, who strolled back into the park where he waited around for it to grow dark. He hesitated a moment before taking off his newly recovered ski jacket. He'd hate to lose it again, so he made sure it and his other clothes were well hidden before making the shift.

After shifting into the owl form, he decided to fly around a bit before settling down to hunt for his evening meal. The air was crisp and clean for being in the city, and the lights below sparkled in multiple shades of white, yellow and gold. He could see the citizens of Asheville rushing to their cars to get home to their warm homes and families. Everyone was too busy to bother looking up, so he was able to fly around without being noticed. After a few minutes, he returned to the darkened part of the park where the hunting was best.

In the space of a couple of hours, he was able to kill two rabbits and a squirrel. That should be enough to get him into the gathering. Not exactly like bringing a bottle of wine to a party, he thought, but under the circumstances, the fresh game might be preferred over booze. Besides, as he'd learned on his first day, without proper ID one's shopping choices were significantly curtailed as was one's ability to make money so you could afford to go shopping.

After making the last kill, he dragged it to where he'd stashed the others, shifting back to human form and quickly dressing. He relished putting on the ski jacket and feeling the warmth start to build inside of it. He cleaned the game, being careful not to get blood on the coat, then stuck the carcasses in a bag before hiding the makeshift bottle knife. Sure would be nice if he could somehow get his knife and other belongings back. Maybe he'd talk to Luke about that. See if he could negotiate with this Saul fellow.

Okay, time to find the party, he thought as he pulled the directions he'd scribbled down. The day had turned out alright after all.

3

LESS THAN TWENTY-FOUR hours later, Pat was back on the phone with Shack.

"I've got some more news, and it's not good...not good at all," Shack said straight away without even a hint of flirting first, which immediately set off Pat's alarm bells.

"What is it, Shack?"

"I've tracked down the knife; at least where it was as of yesterday evening."

"Okay, that's a good start," Pat replied. "Where was it?"

"Apparently cutting a couple of homeless people's throats," Shack replied.

"What? Impossible! TJ would never do such a thing." *At least I don't think he would,* Pat thought.

"Here's what happened as best as I can make out. I have a cop who owes me a couple of favors, so the story's source is strong. The police were called out to an alley behind one of the homeless shelters around 9 pm. It seems there had been an altercation. One of the shelter employees heard a ruckus outside and called them. When they arrived, they found a homeless man dead and his female companion bleeding out. They'd both had their throats cut. They managed to stop her bleeding in time to save her, but it appears her vocal chords may have been damaged. That part isn't clear. She may have been mute before the incident. Anyway, the two were identified as Saul Young and Sally Morrow. I know both of them, or at least their street rep. They're both bad apples. Whoever took them out probably did the city a big favor."

"How do they know my knife was involved?" Pat asked.

"Sally isn't able to talk, but she was able to draw. It turns out she's not a bad artist. She drew two pictures; one of a knife and one of a teenage boy then drew a line between the two. My cop friend took a picture with his cellphone and sent it to me. Sorry to say, the pictures fit your knife and boy to a T. I'll forward it on to you when I get off."

Pat sat down on the kitchen chair, the tea she was in the process of fixing forgotten. What in the hell was she going to do now? Surely it was just a matter of time before the cops tracked TJ down and then the shit was going to hit the fan. Now, it was more important than ever for her to find him, but then what? Her brain was swirling but without any solution coming to mind, a little like a computer searching for a file that simply wasn't on the hard drive. She suddenly realized Shack had asked her a question.

"What was that again?"

"I said, what do you want me to do now?"

"Find TJ before the cops do," Pat replied, an idea starting to form. "And one more thing, Shack. Do you still have that connection with the guy who prepares fake IDs?"

"Yeeaaahh..." Shack replied slowly. "I might be able to help you out there. Why?"

Gathering

As TJ followed Luke's directions to the gathering, he wondered if the old man had sent him on a wild goose chase. He found himself walking through a well-manicured residential neighborhood that seemed to TJ to be an unlikely setting for a gathering of homeless people. He felt self-conscious strolling along the streets with his plastic bag of recently killed game. He could imagine people inside their homes staring at him before rushing to their phones to call the cops. Still, he didn't have anything else to do with his time, and Luke had appeared genuine with his invitation, so he'd keep walking at least until the patrol cars arrived.

Luckily none did, and as he continued to walk the houses grew sparser, and within a few blocks, he found himself in a wooded area not yet taken over by the urban sprawl. As he followed the roadway around an outcropping of trees, he heard the sound of music in the distance and detected a scent that started his mouth to water with anticipation. Walking a little further, he saw a clearing up ahead with lights fluttering through the trees in the distance. These turned out to be from fires burning inside some large metal drums. Around each fire people stood and sat, many of them swaying to the music that came from a boombox TJ figured was probably close to twenty years old.

He suddenly felt awkward walking into such a gathering, but then relaxed as he saw Precious bounding towards him, her tongue flapping to one side like a welcome flag. Her limp appeared much better, and she seemed no worse for her adventure earlier in the day. As she reached him, she reared up on her hind legs and pawed the air with her front, obviously pleased to see him. Luke followed close behind, much more calmly but with a smile on his face as well.

"Welcome to our gathering, TJ. Come, let me introduce you to some of my family."

"You have family here?" TJ asked as he once again accepted Luke's outstretched gnarled hand in greeting.

"Yep, the best kind of family — people I've chosen to be part of my life," Luke replied. "And don't worry about remembering the names. You'll get to learn them if you stay around long enough. Hell, some of us have trouble remembering our own names these days."

TJ appreciated the warning, for within minutes he had more names and faces swirling around than he had any hope of making sense. Peggy Sue (was she the one with the red and pink hair?), Elmer Fudd (could that have really been his name?), Alley Cat (pretty sure she was the young, cute one but with the much bigger boy holding her hand), and the names and faces went on. Everyone appeared to welcome him with open arms and graciously accepted his donation to the stew that was in process.

"Let me help by cutting these into chunks," Luke said as he reached into the faded green coat with the multiple pockets and brought out a large hunting knife in a leather sheath — the knife that Pat had given TJ for his birthday.

TJ stood there staring at the knife as Luke took it out of its sheath and started to reach for the bag of game, a crooked smile beginning to play on his face.

"That's my knife." TJ finally managed to get the words out. "Where did you...?"

"Is it now?" Luke replied. "You know what they say..."

"Yeah," TJ replied with a dejected tone in his voice. "Possession is nine-tenths of the law."

"You're learning quickly, my boy," Luke replied, "Except in this case it's not true." He flipped the knife in the air, deftly grabbing the sharp end and offering the handle end to TJ.

"Several of us have pretty much had it with Saul and Sally's antics recently. Giving our little town here a bad name, so we had an 'intervention.' Under the circumstances, I'd say they were quite understanding. They both wanted to be sure you got what they 'borrowed' from you the other day."

As TJ took the knife from him, Luke reached into another of his many pockets and pulled out the CD case of TJ's video game and Mimi's book. "I believe these are yours as well. Unfortunately, they'd already hocked the backpack and clothes, but if you're not too particular about your fashion tastes, we can hunt you up some more clothes in the next day or two, but not until we get you washed up."

"How will you do that?" TJ asked. "I thought about washing off in the fountain at the park, but the idea of jumping into that frigid water was a little too much."

"Not to mention that some Big Blue would likely arrest you for indecent exposure," Luke added with a chuckle.

"Big Blue?"

"Yeah, that's what we call the cops around here. For the most part, they leave us alone as long as we don't do anything stupid," Luke replied.

"Like trying to wash in the fountain?" TJ asked.

"Exactly," Luke answered. "No, most of us use the shelter over on Patton Avenue. The shower stalls are clean, they seldom run out of hot water, and the staff there don't try to save your soul...least not too often. Of course, there's no point in cleaning yourself up just to put you back in those nasty clothes or to send you back to sleep in a dumpster."

"Yeah, that's been my dilemma," TJ admitted. "I wasn't figuring on getting mugged my first night. I'm afraid I didn't have a plan B when that happened, but I'm learning."

Luke threw his head back and laughed heartily. "I bet you are. The street is a good teacher if it doesn't kill you in the process. Most of us will spend the night here. There's plenty of wood to keep the fires stoked, and I don't expect Big Blue will be visiting us. If so, hightail it to those woods over there, and we'll meet up tomorrow in the same area we met today."

"What is this area, anyway?" TJ asked. It was fully dark by now and impossible to see more than a few yards beyond the light of the fires.

"It's a construction site," Luke replied as he took a pocket knife from his coat pocket and began cutting up one of the rabbits with it. "In a couple of weeks they'll finish paving the roads, and a few months after that, there will be rows of new houses. Jacob over there has been doing some work for the contractor and promised to clean up a lot of trash left over from the initial clearing, which is where the fires come in. We're staying warm and cleaning up all at the same time."

"Wow, that's cool," TJ said.

"Yeah, I just wished more people were willing to give us a chance. Of course, then you run into folks like Saul and Sally who end up giving the rest of us a bad rep. It can become a downward spiral if you let it."

TJ thought about what Luke said. He had sure gotten himself stuck in such a spiral. "You seem to have a pretty good outlook on life," he finally said. "How do you manage it?"

Luke looked up from his work and stared into the fire for a moment before finally answering. "I spent quite a bit of time in Vietnam when I was in the service. That's where this came from." He held up the hand without the two fingers. "I learned a little about karma from one of the Buddhist priests I met there. It took me years to get the hang of it...probably still fail more often than not, but it seems to work for me."

"Karma?" TJ asked as he pulled the other rabbit from the bag. "You mentioned that before, but I haven't a clue what you're talking about."

"I'm probably not the best one to teach it to you," Luke replied, "but this is my take on it in its simplest terms — what goes around, comes around. I had it tattooed on my arm so I wouldn't forget it." He pushed up the sleeve of his left arm to reveal the words inscribed in a circle on his arm.

"Wow, couldn't you just have written it on a piece of paper and kept it in your pocket?" TJ asked.

Luke threw his head back and laughed for a second time. "Maybe, but it wouldn't have meant the same thing."

"But what does it mean—what goes around comes around?"

"Here's how I think of it," Luke replied as he cut off a chunk of meat from the hind quarter of the rabbit and popped it in his mouth. "The results of things that one has done will someday affect the person who started the events. Take Saul and Sally, for example. They've been doing some pretty bad stuff to people. You're not the first one to fall for their scheme. They've been sowing some pretty bad 'karmic seeds,' and earlier today they reaped the results."

"What did you do to them?" TJ asked, suddenly worried.

"Let's just say my friends, and I helped keep the karmic wheel turning." Luke rotated one finger around, outlining the circle of words on his arm. "Now, finish cutting up your rabbit and let's get it in the pot. People are getting hungry."

As the two of them walked over to the large pot of simmering stew, TJ said, "You realize you ate some of that rabbit raw?"

"Did I now?" Luke said as he tossed a small chunk of it to Precious before popping another piece in his mouth. "Guess I learned that from ole Precious here. You learn to appreciate all the bounty this Earth has to offer in whatever form it comes to you."

Soul Searching

1

It took a couple of sleepless nights and more soul searching than Pat could remember ever doing before, but she felt like she finally had a plan that she could live with if she could pull it off. She had come to the conclusion she somehow needed to get TJ out of Allan and her lives if they were to have any chance of making it as a couple. At the same time, she had grown too fond of TJ to simply ruin his life by turning him over to Oliver and his crew at B.I.U.F.O. She had to give the boy the opportunity to find his place in the world—as long as that place didn't involve Allan or her.

So far, she'd managed to be vague with Allan whenever he asked how the search for TJ was coming along; a question he asked her several times a day. But she wasn't sure how much longer she could keep him in the dark before he decided to take some action on his own. As it turned out, she was assisted by a busier than usual time at the clinic.

While she waited to hear back from Shack, Pat resorted to numerous long walks through the woods. It was during one such walk that she received the call from the Asheville P.I.

"What you got for me?" she asked.

"Good news!" Shack replied. "At least some of it is good. The documents you requested are ready, but the price tag is pretty high. Rushed jobs always cost more..."

"Not a problem," Pat interrupted him. "I figured as much. What's the quality like?"

"Good," Shack replied. "They should work just fine."

"And the other news? Good or bad?" Pat asked.

"I'd say a little of both. The cops are continuing to look for the boy, but so far the case is still low on their priority list. After all, a homeless kid knocking off a couple of other homeless people isn't that big a deal to them, and they're trying to keep a low profile on it. It's not the kind of story any of the powers-that-be want to hit the newsstand, especially as we start the holiday shopping season."

"Any word on the Sally woman's condition?"

"She's out of I.C.U. and is expected to recover, but she's still not able to talk."

"Okay, thanks for keeping me up to date," Pat said. "How do I go about getting those documents?"

"Glad you asked," Shack replied with a lighter tone in his voice. "Remember that steak and seafood restaurant I mentioned the other day?"

Pat groaned but with a smile trying to break the surface of her face, something that hadn't shown up there in several days. "Yeah, I remember."

"We have reservations for 7 p.m. tonight...in your name. I'll have the papers with me. Bring the cash — five G's in small bills. And oh, do you still have that black, sequin gown you wore to that Gala a few years ago? I'd love to see you in that again."

2

"GUESS WHAT?" MIMI SHOUTED to Kendra as she ran up to her outside their school, drawing the attention of several other kids who were also leaving the school grounds late.

Kendra hadn't seen her friend so excited or animated in quite some time, not since receiving the decree from her father that she could no longer help TJ with his homeschooling.

"I don't know, but I bet you're going to tell me, right?"

"You bet I am," Mimi said as she hugged Kendra, spinning the two of them around until Kendra felt like they'd end up falling to the ground.

"Whoa there. Not so enthusiastic," but she couldn't help but laugh. It was good to see Mimi happy again. "So what's got you so excited?"

"I just came from the D.M.V., and I passed my driver's license test! I got my license!" Mimi said as she finally let go of her friend.

"Wow! That is good news," Kendra replied. "I thought your dad wouldn't let you get one."

"Yeah, he wouldn't for the longest time, but Uncle Bo and I finally persuaded him to let me try for it. I think dear old Dad figured his dumb daughter would never pass the test, but I did!"

"Congratulations," Kendra said. "That's quite an accomplishment."

"Yeah, I guess so," Mimi replied, "but don't you realize what this means?"

"That you're not nearly as dumb as your dad thinks?" Kendra guessed.

"Well, yeah, that too, but what it means is that we can now go find TJ." And with that Mimi started her happy dance again.

"What? You're kidding. Pat said he'd run away to Asheville. That's over thirty miles away."

"Yeah, thirty-two miles to be exact," Mimi replied. "I looked it up yesterday during my study break. So, we don't have to walk now. We can drive."

"Huh, just one little detail. To take such a trip requires more than just a driver's license. We'd also need a car."

"I know that silly," Mimi replied undaunted by Kendra's lack of enthusiasm. "Uncle Bo won't lend me his truck. Hell, he won't even let his brother drive it, but he's had an old clunker of a car in the barn for ages. He got it running the other day and said I could use it."

"To go all the way to Asheville?"

"I'm not going to tell him where we're going," Mimi admitted. "You know the old saying, 'Sometimes it better to ask for forgiveness than for permission.' This is one of those times."

"Okay," Kendra replied, starting to warm to the idea. "I guess we're going on our first road trip to Asheville. When do we leave?"

"Early tomorrow morning. Uncle Bo gets up at the crack of dawn to go hunting on Saturdays this time of the year, so we can get an early start as well. I'll pick you up around 7."

"In the morning?" Kendra asked, suddenly less excited by the idea. She'd planned to sleep in since her sitting and homeschool job was temporarily on hold.

"Of course in the morning," Mimi said. "That way we'll have all day to find TJ and bring him home where he belongs."

"Okay, I guess," Kendra said. She knew it was pointless to try to talk her friend out of one of her ideas once it took hold. "Maybe we can get some early Christmas shopping in while we're there."

"There's only one thing I want for Christmas," Mimi replied. "And that's TJ."

Kendra studied her friend's face, looking for clues about what that last comment meant, but Mimi just smiled innocently back as she added, "That is, I want him back home where he belongs. For Allan and Pat's sake."

Menial Job

It had been a week since TJ had been serendipitously introduced to Luke through his dog, Precious, but much had happened during that time. For starters, Luke had taken TJ to the Salvation Army for a set of hand-me-down clothes and then on to the homeless shelter. There TJ enjoyed a thorough cleaning followed by a hot meal.

Things are beginning to look up, TJ thought, as he glanced around the dining hall that was about eighty percent filled with other homeless people and others down on their luck. As Luke had been quick to point out, "We live in a pretty great country that provides such accommodations and resources for less fortunate people."

The comment surprised TJ coming from an old Army vet who seemed to have been given the short end of the stick by his country.

"No, not at all," Luke disagreed. "This country has been good to me. Oh, I know it has its faults, don't get me wrong. I'd like to see veterans treated with more respect, and for sure the VA department needs a major overhauling. It's like my old lieutenant used to say, 'We're not perfect, just better than any of the alternatives.'"

Next, TJ learned from Luke that there were some jobs available that didn't require ID papers or written permission from a parent. They were menial jobs like unloading trucks, or at other times of the year, picking apples, and the like. Most of them paid below minimum wage for hard, back-breaking work, but you got paid at the end of the day in cash. Such work was spotty at best, but TJ had been lucky that morning and obtained his first such job. Now, although he was bone tired, it felt good to have a few bucks in his pocket. He planned to pay Luke back the money he'd given him, but that still left some money over for food. He figured he'd surprise Luke and the others with sandwiches from Subway, his treat in thanks for all they'd done for him.

Of course, he'd had to show the young lady behind the sandwich counter that he had enough money to pay for the sandwiches before she'd make them for him, but it would take more than that to dampen his spirit this evening. He grabbed the bag of sandwiches and headed to his new family's latest location.

They'd stayed at the construction site for three nights before they had to move on. He'd learned that it was safer to not stay at any one location for more than two or three days. Their latest location was at a small park known as the Bountiful Cities Edible Gardens, though in November there wasn't anything edible on the grounds as far as TJ could tell. Still, it wasn't far from Pack Square Park, where he liked to hang out during the day, and Luke had told him that it was a pretty safe place to bed down for a couple of nights.

"We should be fine as long as we keep the fire small and the boom box on low," Luke had said.

By the time TJ arrived, Luke and Precious were already there along with Alley Cat and her boyfriend, Oscar, as well as Elmer and a new family member Luke introduced as Marlin. "He loves fish and smells like one that's been kept out in the sun for about three days most of the time," Luke said by way of introduction, then noticing the bag asked, "Whatcha brung us?"

"Sandwiches from Subway," TJ said, holding the bag up for everyone to see.

"So you got the job, huh?"

"Yeah, and they paid me at the end just like you said they would."

"Good," Luke replied as he pulled one of the sandwiches from the bag. "You didn't need to spend all your money trying to feed us though."'

"I know, but I wanted to," TJ replied as he tossed a couple of the other sandwiches to Alley Cat and Oscar. "Besides, I still have a few bucks left over."

Everyone sat around the fire that Luke had built, munching quietly on the food. Finally, Luke looked over at TJ with a serious look on his face.

"How old are you, boy?"

Not knowing how to answer the question TJ answered, "Old enough."

"Do you have your high school diploma?"

"What's that?" TJ asked, taking the last bite from his sandwich, then tossing the paper into the fire.

"It's what you get when you graduate from high school," Luke replied. "Everyone knows that."

"I was homeschooled," TJ replied a little defensively. "Why all the questions?"

"Oh, I was just wondering what your plans were?" Luke replied after a moment.

"Plans?" TJ studied his new friend with a puzzled look on his face. "I don't know. I guess I plan to sleep here tonight and maybe go looking for another day job tomorrow."

"And after that?" Luke persisted.

"Hell, I don't know," TJ replied, suddenly irritated, mostly at himself because he'd been avoiding asking himself such questions.

The two of them sat quietly. Luke rubbed Precious's ear as she lay sleeping beside him, snoring quietly. Now and then he'd toss a twig into the fire. Finally, he said, "I noticed that game you have was called *Mercenaries*. You any good at it?"

"Not bad," TJ replied, though he knew he was one of the best players around, at least from what he'd read on the internet from other gamers.

"Well, playing a game ain't the same thing as being in a real war," Luke said, "but I was wondering if you ever thought about joining the Army. Sure beats working those day jobs for next to nothing."

"You trying to get rid of me?" TJ asked, only partly joking.

"Nah, that ain't it. I'm just saying a body could do a lot worse, especially someone who didn't have anything better planned. Think about it." And with that he lay back, pulling his faded green Army jacket around him and went to sleep.

Piece of Work

1

Two days after meeting Shack in Asheville to pick up TJ's fake ID papers, Pat received another call from the P.I.

"Wow! I can't believe you're calling me on a Saturday morning and before noon," Pat joked with him.

"I can't believe it either," Shack replied in a less than spritely voice, "but I just received word from one of my street connections. I think we may have found your boy."

"Really! That's good to hear," Pat replied. "Where is he?"

"My connection says that he's seen a boy that fits the description hanging around the Pack Square Park area. Seems like he's hooked up with an old Army vet named Luke Glover. If so, that's probably a good thing. I know Luke. He's not a bad guy."

"Okay, that's good to hear," Pat repeated.

"That's the good news," Shack continued. "The not so good news is that I've also heard that a local reporter has gotten wind of the throat slashing incident and is investigating it. He's been snooping around as well and could break the story at any time."

"Damn," Pat said.

"He's not the most ethical guy. You may be able to pay for his silence."

Pat groaned. Her savings account had already taken a significant hit with the purchase of the I.D. papers, but she could hardly be concerned with the cost at this point.

"Okay, see what you can do to keep him quiet for at least the next few days. I'm coming over. I can be there within the hour."

"I thought that might be the case," Shack replied less than enthusiastically. "Bring coffee, plenty of coffee. Here's the address of the park where we can meet."

After getting the address, Pat hung up the phone, pulled a thermos out of the kitchen cabinet and poured the remaining pot of coffee in it. She double checked her bag that looked like a cross between a briefcase and a purse to be sure the I.D. papers were inside, then quickly scribbled a note to Allan that she'd gone shopping. He would receive it later in the day when he returned from his half day at the clinic. She then grabbed her car keys and flew out the door.

She found Shack slouching on one of the park benches dressed in a trench coat and with a black felt hat covering his face. As she approached, Pat could hear him snoring softly.

"I brought the coffee," she said as she sat down beside him and took the thermos out of her satchel.

"Can you just shoot it into me intravenously?" Shack asked from under his hat.

"Sorry, but I left my I.V. set at home," Pat replied. "But here's a cup." She poured the coffee into the top of the thermos and placed it into Shack's hand. "Careful, it's still pretty hot."

Shack pushed the hat from his face and onto his head as he sat up. "Bless you, my child," he said, looking at Pat for the first time. "And while I'm at it, I want to thank you for a lovely evening the other night. One I will never forget. You're really quite amazing, as I knew you would be."

"You do recall that I didn't go home with you despite your many invitations?"

"Oh sure, I know," Shack replied. "I knew you never would. That really wasn't the point, anyway."

"And what, pray tell, was the point?"

"For us to be seen in public," Shack replied.

"Yes, well you certainly accomplished that. I don't recall a time when my dinner was interrupted more often."

"Yes, exactly," Shack said as he took a sip of the coffee and, finding it not so hot, he took a long slurp. "Why, I already have three other dates from three different women—women that previously wouldn't have given me the time of day."

Pat chuckled despite herself. "You know, Shack, you are one piece of work."

"Thanks," Shack replied.

"That wasn't intended as a compliment."

"I know, but that's how I'm choosing to take it. Now onto the business at hand."

"Yes, please. I can tell you've been scoping out the area before I arrived," Pat said sarcastically.

"Actually, yes, I did, just before taking a nap so I'd be fully alert for your arrival." He pointed across the park. "He's over there."

2

"I FEEL LIKE WE'RE TWO country bumpkins come to the big city," Kendra said, sweeping her arms out to take in the crowded sidewalk and streets before her.

"I know what you mean," Mimi agreed. "It's been well over a year since I've visited Asheville. I didn't realize it had grown so much."

"We'll never find TJ," Kendra lamented. "It's like trying to find a needle in a haystack. We've been walking around for close to three hours now, and I haven't seen anyone who even remotely looks like him."

"True," Mimi said, "but we have seen a few dreamy guys."

Kendra stopped in the middle of the sidewalk and stared at her friend. "Are you in heat?"

"No," Mimi snapped back defensively. "Least, I don't think so."

"Let's take a break and get a bite to eat on me," Kendra said. "How's that place look?"

"Looks fine to me."

They had beaten the lunch crowd, so it was easy to find a table. As they sat down, Mimi placed the picture of TJ on the table. They'd been showing it around to folks on the off chance someone may have seen him. So far, no one had.

A young woman with her blonde hair tied back in a ponytail came out from the kitchen with a tray of food. After delivering it to two couples sitting at a nearby table, she walked over to them.

"Have you had a chance to look at the menu yet? I can also go over our lunch specials if you like."

"Those sandwiches you just delivered look delicious," Kendra said. "What are they?"

"Those are one of our restaurant's specialties. They're Rubens but with a special sauce that most people say make the sandwich extra special."

Kendra looked at her friend. "What say we split one of those?"

"Sounds good to me. And I just want water to drink...lots of water."

The waitress started to turn away but then stopped when she noticed the picture lying on the table.

"You know him?" she asked, pointing down at the picture.

"Why, yes," Mimi replied. "He's a friend of ours. We've been looking for him all morning but so far, no luck. Why? Do you recognize him?"

The waitress picked up the picture to take a closer look before replying. "Yeah, that's him. He's a lot cleaner in this picture, but he's definitely the one who came in here several days ago looking for a job."

"Really? Did you give him one?" Kendra asked.

"Nah, couldn't do it. He didn't have any ID proving his age, not to mention the fact that he smelled like the town dump."

"Darn!" Mimi said, clearly disappointed. "We're back to square one."

The waitress started back to the kitchen, then stopped and returned to the table. "You might try Pack Square Park. It's just a few blocks from here. It's a pretty popular place for...for folks down on their luck. I'll draw you a map before you leave."

"Thanks. That would be great," Mimi said, a note of hope returning to her voice.

After the waitress left, she turned to Kendra. "This is a sign. Our luck is about to change. I feel certain of it."

"I sure hope so," Kendra replied. "I'm not sure how much more walking my poor feet can take."

Cheerios

"Catch!" The word shook TJ out of a warm, sun-induced stupor. Like a cat who's unexpectedly awakened from a catnap, TJ jerked his head up just in time to see a bag of Cheerios flying towards his head. Without a thought or a moment of hesitation, he snatched it out of the air with one hand, then looked around to find its source.

Pat Vogt stood about ten feet away, a smile on her face.

"You've always had amazing reflexes," she said as she stepped forward. She was wearing a stylish navy blue overcoat with a matching handbag hung over one shoulder. For just a moment, TJ had a warm glow of recognition come over him. It was good to see a familiar face. He felt a smile start on his face but then froze in place as he remembered the late night conversation from a couple of weeks ago.

"How about coming with me to get some milk to go with those?" she asked, pointing to the bag in his hand.

"I'd rather have coffee," he replied, trying to keep his voice low so it would sound as adult as possible. After all, adulthood wasn't far off. Just the other day he'd felt along his chin and was surprised to feel the first evidence of whiskers on his otherwise youthful face.

"Okay, coffee it is," Pat replied.

As TJ started to stand, he heard Precious' low growl of warning. He glanced over to where she stood next to Luke, both of them watching him closely.

"It's okay," TJ said, holding up a hand towards Precious. "She's a..." *Friend? Not really. My mom? No.* "She's someone I know. I'll be back in a little while."

Luke nodded as he reached out and patted Precious to assure her as well.

"We'll be right here if you need anything. Best coffee in town is at Double D's over on Biltmore. Just look for the double-decker bus," Luke said.

The two of them walked along in the direction Luke had indicated, neither of them saying a word. They found Double-D's without any difficulty. Sure enough, it was located in a red vintage double-decker bus that looked like it belonged on the streets of London more than in a Southern town. Despite the chilly temperatures of December, they decided to sit outside where there were fewer people and at least the illusion of privacy.

After the wait person took their order for two large coffees, TJ thought about asking Pat how she'd managed to find him, but then realized he really didn't want to know, and he wasn't in the mood for small talk anyway.

Evidently, neither was Pat who, after a couple of minutes of awkward silence, opened her handbag and took out a large business sized envelope and pushed it towards him.

"What's that?" TJ asked without picking it up.

"It's your pass to a new life," Pat replied, then went on to explain. "It's a set of ID papers—driver's license, birth certificate and a social security card all in your name or a name that you can adopt."

"Really?" TJ asked, suddenly interested despite himself. He picked up the envelope and opened it. He pulled out the largest piece of paper, which turned out to be a birth certificate.

"Todd John Jacobs," Todd read the name on the certificate. Jacobs? Where had she gotten that name and why did it sound familiar. Then he remembered. It was the last name of his favorite character in *Mercenaries*. He looked at Pat now for the first time since they'd arrived at the coffee shop, a quizzical look on his face.

"I did my research," Pat said.

TJ nodded and then looked into the envelope. It had felt heavier than he'd expected it to when he picked it up, and now he realized why. Along with two laminated cards was a one-inch stack of money held together by a thick rubber band. He could just make out that the top bill was a fifty. It was more money than he'd ever seen. He placed the certificate back in the envelope and dropped it on the table.

"What is this all about?" he finally asked. "Are you trying to bribe me to come home?"

"No," Pat replied, shaking her head. "As I said, this is your passport to a new life, one that doesn't involve Allan or me."

TJ nodded as he continued to study the envelope. "And what if I decline your generous and manipulative invitation?"

"You don't understand. This isn't an invitation. It's a demand. Take it or else."

"Or else what?" TJ shot back, feeling his hackles rise along the back of his neck.

"Remember my phone conversation the night you left?" Pat asked.

"Yes," TJ said.

"That was to my friend, Oliver. He works for B.I.U.F.O. - The Bureau of Investigation for Unidentified Flying Objects."

"So?" TJ asked. "Why would he care anything about me?"

Pat stared at him before finally answering. "Don't you know what you are? What Homlin was?"

"No," TJ replied, a puzzled look growing on his face. He had to admit he'd wondered about that—a lot lately, as he realized how different he was from everyone else.

Pat continued to study his face, finally deciding she believed he was telling the truth. He really didn't know...but how to break it to him? Was that really her job, her role in this game? She'd always believed that the direct approach was best. She'd learned it from her father while still a young girl.

"Homlin was not of this Earth," Pat said, looking straight at TJ to monitor his reaction. "While it's not yet been determined where he came from, it's very clear that he was an alien, and you are a product of what he brought with him."

TJ blinked several times as he processed her comments, finally replying, "So, you're saying that I'm an alien as well. Is that right?"

Pat nodded. "Yes, that's correct." There, it was out in the open now. Suddenly she felt a great weight lifted off her chest.

TJ continued to sit there with a blank look on his face. Then slowly he smiled. "You know, that explains a lot—a whole lot." The smile grew into a wide grin.

Pat watched him, surprised by his reaction to the news.

"Homlin is no longer a threat to this world. He's been neutralized, and his plan for world domination stopped," Pat continued. "I can't go into any more detail than that without breaking a sacred pledge, but I will say this. I don't believe you are a threat to this world; at least not at the level that Homlin was.

While you are the product of his devious plan, I do not believe you are devious. Allan raised you as his son and as a human being, and I respect that. I've grown too fond of you, TJ, to simply turn you over to Oliver. I want to give you this chance, but if you refuse, then I'll have no other option but to turn you in."

TJ sat there staring at the envelope, considering what Pat had said. Finally, he picked the envelope back up and removed the birth certificate. He read the date of birth, then looked at Pat.

"This would make me eighteen...today. Today is my birthday?"

"Yeah, that's right, and this is your birthday present from Allan and me." She reached out and grasped his hand. He started to pull it away but then stopped. "At eighteen, you can get a job without permission from a parent or guardian. You can do a lot at eighteen, so I figured..."

"No, no, that's fine," TJ interrupted. "That's great. Now I can get a job." But it wasn't a job he was thinking about, at least not a job in Asheville. He'd been thinking about what Luke had said a few days ago about joining the Army. Now he had the paperwork he needed and even the last name of his favorite mercenary. Maybe Pat was right. This was the start of a whole new life.

He had walked by the Army Recruiting Station over on Oak Street a number of times, but so far hadn't had the nerve to walk in, but now he could. He could go in with his head held high with a new name and proof of his age. TJ reached out with his other hand and placed it over Pat's. He patted it gently.

"Thanks," he said with as much sincerity as he could muster. "I hope I never see you again," he added with the same sincerity. He rose from the table and picked up the envelope. He stuck it in his coat as he walked away, leaving Pat alone at the table.

Papers

1

As TJ walked back to Pack Square Park with the envelope secured away in his jacket, he felt an emotional storm brewing within. On the one hand, he was excited about the new life that lay before him as Todd John Jacobs, future mercenary extraordinaire. On the other hand, he felt a blanket of sadness trying to descend upon him at the thought of never seeing Allan again. Not only Allan, TJ realized, but also Kendra and Mimi would now be out of his life as well. Had he made the best bargain he could? He really hadn't been in a position to bargain or negotiate. He had known Pat long enough to know that she rarely if ever bluffed. If she said she'd report him to her friend at B.I.U.F.O., he knew she meant business.

And while he was cutting the cord from his past, he might as well go all out and say goodbye to Luke and Precious. He'd checked the schedule posted on the front door of the recruiting station, and he knew it was open on Saturdays. He found the two of them where he'd left them basking in the midday sunshine of the park. TJ noticed Luke's box with the flag sticking out of it had more money than usual. Evidently, the sunny skies had brought more people out to the park. As TJ approached, Luke looked up at him from where he sat crossed legged on a cushion he carried around for that purpose.

"Everything okay?" Luke asked.

"Yeah, it's cool," TJ replied as he sat down beside him and reached out to scratch behind Precious' ear. "She's a...a friend of the family. She brought me some papers from home."

"Papers?" Luke asked. "What kind of papers?"

"ID papers."

"What you need with those?"

"I've been thinking about what you said the other day when you asked me about what my plans were. I realized I didn't have any plans beyond getting away from home and getting settled here in Asheville."

Luke nodded. "And now?"

"And now I have a plan," TJ continued. "I'm going to join the Army as you suggested."

Luke nodded again, this time with a slight smile appearing on his face behind his beard and mustache. "You could do worse," he said. "You could really screw up and join the Navy or, God forbid, the Air Force. So that's what you needed with the ID papers."

"Yeah, that's right."

"And now you've come to say goodbye. Is that it?"

"Yeah, that's about the size of it." Suddenly, TJ felt a tightness in his chest. In the short time he'd been in Asheville, he'd grown fond of the old man and dog. "I mean, I can wait a day or two if you'd rather..."

"No," Luke said abruptly, then repeated in a softer tone. "No, it's good timing. If I were you, I wouldn't wait."

TJ sat there considering what Luke had said. "What do you mean, it's good timing?"

Luke reached into his coat pocket and brought out a crumpled piece of paper and handed it to him.

TJ unfolded it and studied it for a moment before looking up. "This looks like a drawing of me, and if I'm not mistaken, that must be my knife. Where did you get it?"

"Big Blue has been passing them around among the homeless," Luke replied. "They're looking for you, but want to keep it quiet and out of the public's eye if possible."

"What? Why?" TJ asked feeling a different type of tightness building. He noticed Luke looking down, avoiding him. "What is this about? Is this about Saul and Sally? Did they report me to the police or something?"

"No," Luke replied, still not able to look at TJ. "Not exactly...though it does involve Saul and Sally." He pulled the box of money towards him and pretended to count his take for the day, but TJ could tell he wasn't really counting it. Finally Luke looked up at him.

"Me and some of the other guys went to talk to Saul and Sally to try to persuade them to give back your stuff and stop scamming people, but things went bad. Saul had been drinking and, boy is he a mean drunk. He started yelling and screaming. Then he took out your knife and came for me with Sally right behind him. I guess I must have gone into counter-attack mode. I'm not too clear what happened after that. Next thing I knew, a couple of the guys were washing my hands and face, and the cloth kept coming away all bloody."

"What did you do? Why are they looking for me? I haven't done anything."

"I know, I know. The guys told me that I freaked out when Saul and Sally came at me—went all commando on them. They told me that I killed both of them, but they were wrong. I killed Saul, but Sally survived. She isn't able to talk, so she drew this picture. No one knows why for sure. Sally has always been a bit touched in the head. Big Blue put two and two together..."

"And came up with five," TJ finished. "They came to the wrong conclusion."

"It's not the first time," Luke said. After a long pause, he continued. "If you want, I'll turn myself in. I'll explain what happened and maybe..." The last words hung in the air unfinished.

"You can't do that," TJ replied. "They'll put you away for the rest of your life. I couldn't live with myself. Hell, you were just trying to help me get my stuff back." He looked down at the paper again. "But you're right. I need to get the hell out of here—fast."

Luke nodded, then reached inside his shirt and removed a set of dog tags. He held them out to TJ. "Give these to the recruiter over on Oak Street. It'll either be Starr or Lee. Every once in awhile I'll send them someone I feel would make a good soldier. I have a pretty good track record. They'll treat you right. Tell them I'm asking them to expedite your process."

TJ took the tags from him and dropped them in the envelope, then pulled a few of the bills from the stack of money and handed them to Luke who just stared at it.

"Take it," TJ said. "Someone told me once not to let my pride get in the way when someone offers to help out. You need to get yourself out of town for awhile. This will help."

After another moment of hesitation, Luke took the money and dropped it into the box. He studied TJ for a moment.

"Let me do something to earn this. It's important you make a good first impression so we'll start by getting you cleaned up and with some decent looking clothes."

He stood up and clipped the leather leash onto Precious' collar. "First stop, the Salvation Army, then to the shelter for a much-needed bath. Might need to borrow a pair of scissors to trim your hair as well. Why don't you go ahead over to the Salvation Army, and I'll meet you there. There's something I need to take care of, but it shouldn't take long."

TJ agreed, then strolled off in the direction of the store leaving Pack Square Park for the last time.

2

AS MIMI AND KENDRA arrived at Pack Square Park, they realized their search was far from over. The park was larger than expected and filled with people enjoying the sunny weekend day. Mimi decided to show TJ's photo to a young girl with red and pink hair who looked like she might be a permanent resident of the park.

The girl glanced at the photo for a few seconds, then back to Mimi. "Yeah? What about it?" she asked with a suspicious look on her face.

"We're looking for him," Mimi replied simply.

"So?"

"So, can you help us? It's really important. I'm his sister, and our mom is very sick," Mimi lied. "He'd want to know."

"Oh," the girl replied, her look changing to one of concern. "Sorry to hear that. Yeah, I know him. He's over there with Luke and..." She stopped in mid-sentence. "They were over there near the fountain a few minutes ago. I guess they must have left."

Mimi groaned. "Where would they have gone?"

"Oh, probably back to their condo over on Reed Street," the girl replied.

"Really?" Mimi said with renewed hope.

"Of course not," the girl laughed. "What about the word 'homeless' don't you understand?"

Mimi's face turned red, a mixture of embarrassment and anger. She started to take a step towards the homeless girl, but Kendra stepped in front of her and placed a hand on her arm. "Don't," she said. "It's not worth it. We're getting closer. We just need to keep looking."

After a couple of seconds Mimi relaxed and nodded. "Yeah, you're right."

As they turned to leave, the girl spoke up again. "You might try on the other side of the park. Luke likes to change his location about this time of the day. Says it's better for business. I hope you find your friend," she added in a consoling tone. "Look for an old man with an even older looking cocker spaniel."

Mimi and Kendra headed in the direction the girl had pointed. As they approached the other side of the park, Kendra urged them on. "We're getting closer. I just know we are. I can feel it."

"I hope you're right," Mimi replied and a moment later, "There...over there. Isn't that a cocker spaniel?"

Kendra followed where Mimi pointed. "Yeah, looks like one to me, and she seems to belong to that old man sitting under that tree, but where's TJ?"

"There!" Mimi pointed off to the right where a teenage boy with shaggy black hair was waiting to cross the street.

As the two girls started running towards him, Mimi noticed a young woman rising from the park bench where she'd been sitting. She stepped in front of the two girls to block their path.

"Don't." She spoke the one-word command with such authority that it stopped both of them in their tracks. "You need to let him go," the woman added as she reached out and grasped Mimi's arm for emphasis.

"Pat!" Kendra exclaimed. "What are you doing here? We've got to..."

"You need to let him go," Pat repeated more softly this time. "We all need to let him go." She corrected herself.

"Why?" Mimi asked.

"Because TJ needs to find his place in the world. We've all done what we can to prepare him for this next leg of his journey, but we can't take it with him."

"I don't understand," Mimi replied.

"In time you will," Pat said. "For now you'll just have to trust me."

The three of them stood in silence as the light changed, and TJ crossed the street, disappearing into the crowd of other pedestrians.

Rangers

1

Luke watched until TJ was out of sight before turning around and walking in the other direction with Precious following close behind on the leash. They strolled along one of the paths of the park until they were close to the center before leaving the path to enter a thick clump of trees. When he was sure they were out of sight of any prying eyes, Luke sat down cross-legged on the ground, placing the end of the leash under one leg. He glanced around one final time before reaching into the inside pocket of his coat for his pocket knife enclosed in a worn leather case. He pulled the knife out of its case and stared at the scrimshaw picture of two ducks about to land on a lake etched on its surface. Opening the single blade of the knife he carefully held it up to his ear and spoke a series of numbers into it.

Several seconds passed before he heard a muted voice on the other end of the line.

"Yes?"

I have another one for you," Luke said. "Think this one might be special. You'll want to keep a close eye on him. His name is Todd John Jacobs. He'll be coming in through the regular channels."

"Okay," came the simple reply.

Luke nodded. His job was done...for now. He closed the knife and returned it to its case. He looked over at Precious, who lay dozing in front of him. "Let's go get something to eat, Pretty Girl." He slowly unwrapped his legs and stood up. It had been a good day's work.

2

THE NEXT COUPLE OF days were a blur for TJ. On Luke's recommendation, he made sure he took a bath at the shelter and dressed in his nicest clothes.

"If you wear a t-shirt make sure it doesn't say anything obscene or anti-American," Luke had warned. "And give them this address as your current residence." He handed TJ a slip of paper. "Starr or Lee will know it's not real, but they won't say anything since so far I've not given them any rejects. Make sure you're not the first."

After meeting briefly with Sergeant Starr and filling out some preliminary paperwork and presenting his own identifying papers, everything moved into high gear with the next days filled with aptitude tests, a thorough physical exam, and an interview with another officer who went over the various career options currently available to TJ.

"You've scored in the upper ten percentile on your aptitude test, and you're as physically fit as anyone I've seen in the past year, so you've got quite a few options available to you," the career counselor said.

"I saw a poster of someone jumping out of a plane at the recruiting station," TJ said. "What do I have to do to be able to do that?"

He'd remembered in several of the *Mercenaries* game scenarios that his namesake had often started off his clandestine mission by jumping in behind enemy lines. Besides, he already knew he enjoyed flying, though as a bird rather than in a plane.

"So you think you could be a paratrooper?" the sergeant asked.

"Maybe," TJ replied, then added, "Sure, why not? Someone has to do it."

The sergeant smiled and made a couple of notes on the paper in front of him. "Okay, duly noted. If you want to jump out of planes, maybe you should consider becoming a Ranger."

"What's a Ranger?" TJ asked.

"They're elite fighters who go in fast, hit hard, and get out."

That sounded right up Todd Jacob's alley.

Everything became very real when TJ was asked to take the Oath of Enlistment.

"I, Todd John Jacobs, do solemnly swear that I will support and defend the Constitution of the United States against all enemies, foreign and domestic; that I will bear true faith and allegiance to the same; and that I will obey the orders of the President of the United States and the orders of the officers appointed over me, according to regulations and the Uniform Code of Military Justice. So help me God."

It was the last step before he was whisked off to Basic Training.

Epilogue

1

18 months later

Private First Class Todd John Jacobs paused a moment at the top of the stairs, waiting for his name to be called by his commander. He gazed out at the crowd who enjoyed the early spring-like temperatures of mid-March in Fort Benning, Georgia. It seemed like his fellow soon-to-be Rangers had invited all their family members and friends to join the graduation from Ranger School. As far as he could tell, he was the only one without anyone from his past in attendance.

He'd toyed with the idea of calling Allan and inviting him and Kendra to come down, but then quickly rejected the idea. He'd agreed with Pat, and he wasn't about to use this occasion to renege on the deal.

"Our next soldier has the distinct honor of winning two of our most esteemed awards; something that has never been done since the founding of this school over fifty years ago. Private First Class Todd Jacobs has received the Darby Award, which is bestowed on the Ranger that has shown the best tactical and administrative leadership, has the most positive spot reports, and quite frankly has demonstrated being a cut above the rest."

The crowd clapped but stopped when the commander raised his hand.

"And he also receives the Michael Kelso Enlisted Leadership Award. This award, which is selected by the Ranger's peers, is given to the Ranger who has demonstrated outstanding leadership, initiative, and motivation."

After the applause had subsided, the commander looked up from his notes and smiled. "I also have it on good authority that no one goes hungry while part of Private Jacob's team; something many of us are still trying to figure out how he manages. Private Jacobs, please come forward to receive your awards and diploma."

As Todd walked across the stage, the applause resumed, accompanied by several shouts of encouragement from his fellow graduates. Todd felt his face redden with a mixture of embarrassment and pride as he strolled forward. It had been a grueling two months, but it was now over, and he could get on with the business of being a soldier, but not just any soldier. He was now part of one of the most elite groups of fighters on the planet.

After shaking hands with his commander and receiving his diploma and awards, he exited at the other end of the stage. As he walked down the stairs, he noticed an older man in a dark gray business suit standing at the bottom, gazing up at him. He didn't recognize the man, but from the straightness of the man's stance, Todd suspected he had a military background.

"Congratulations, Private Todd," the man said as he held out his hand. As Todd shook it, he took in the graying hair around the temples and crow's nests around the eyes.

"Thank you, sir," Todd replied as he stifled a wince of pain from the firm handshake. "I'm sorry, do I know you?"

"No, least not yet," the man replied with a chuckle as he released Todd's hand. "But an old friend of yours suggested we meet. My name is Phillip Ackerson, but most of my friends just call me Jersey. I wonder if you've given much thought to what's next for you."

"No, can't say that I have," Todd replied. "Just waiting for my next assignment, I guess."

Jersey nodded. "Good. That's what I'm here to talk to you about." He placed a hand on Todd's back and started guiding him away from the stage. "Your Commander-in-chief has a very special assignment for you."

"My Commander-in-chief?" Todd asked, confused by the title.

"Yes, you know, the President of the United States."

"Oh, yeah, right," Todd replied, his face flushing once more with embarrassment. "But what on earth would he want from me? I'm just a good ole boy from the North Carolina mountains."

"That's what we need to talk about," the man answered as he pointed towards a black SUV parked illegally along the curb, its windows tinted black. It looked like it had been pulled from some Hollywood spy movie. "Right this way, if you please," but it was apparent from the man's tone that it wasn't a request, but an order.

Todd glanced over his shoulder to see if he could draw any of his friends' attention.

"Don't worry," the man said, his hand continuing to guide Todd towards the vehicle. "You're in good hands."

The last thing Todd remembered seeing before he was escorted into the SUV was his commander standing on the stage staring at him, a worried look on his face.

2

IT TOOK JAMES ALMOST two years to find a way to bring some semblance of control to his life as a mercenary. Becoming more selective about the missions had helped, as had insisting on knowing more about the other team members, but he knew these were just temporary steps until a better answer came along. It finally came in the form of a complaint.

Over the past year, Jersey had complained to him a couple of times about how stressful his position had become and how he really wanted to get out of the black ops business and into something quieter. When James prodded further, Jersey confessed he longed to retire to some quiet getaway and open his own restaurant.

"Besides, James, a restaurant in the right location can be a pretty good front so I could keep my hands in a bit without them getting cut off. Why do you ask?"

When James suggested he might be interested in assuming Jersey's role, his old friend had responded positively and then added. "This isn't something I'm comfortable talking about on the phone. How about meeting me in person?"

"Sure, where?"

"There's a cozy little restaurant in Bermuda called the Black Horse Tavern that I've been looking at. You can give me your opinion on whether it would be a good investment; kill two birds with one stone as it were."

As James hung up the phone, he thought, *this could be the start of a whole new phase for both of us.*

3

IT STARTED AS A MILD buzzing in the ears. When it persisted, Val went online to learn that such buzzing was fairly common among humans; a condition called tinnitus. Unfortunately, the buzzing grew in frequency and intensity making it next to impossible to ignore. When it started interrupting his sleep, he considered going to a doctor, but then thought better of it. Even though his "Aeo engineered" body had worked fine for the past two years, he wasn't sure if a doctor might be able to detect a difference.

It was after a week of mostly sleepless nights that he realized the second anniversary of when he'd left the cave and entered human society had been the previous week...just about the time the buzzing had begun. During those two years, he had continued to grow rapidly but decided to ignore Aeo's advice to move from family to family. Maude had turned out to be surprisingly easy to manipulate, in part because she was starving for love and attention. Over the many years they'd been married, Harold had grown increasingly reclusive, spending most of his waking hours in his workshop out back, leaving Maude and Val to themselves. It didn't take long for Val's cute and cuddly act to win her over completely.

When Val heard Maude and Harold arguing one night with Harold insisting they turn him over to social services, Val decided to take matters into his own hands. Harold would have to go. The opportunity arose the next day while Harold was working on the second floor of the barn. Val followed him upstairs, knocked the old man unconscious then broke his neck before tossing him out the window to cover it up.

Maude was devastated, but there was no more talk about social services. About a week after Harold's untimely passing, as she tucked Val in bed she said a short prayer thanking God for sending the young boy to help her through this most trying of times.

The next big challenge was when Maude began noticing Val's incredible appetite and growth. At first, she chalked it up as a growth spurt that many children experience, but when it persisted week in and week out, she became concerned. When she called to book an appointment with the local pediatrician, Val threw such a temper tantrum that she finally hung up the phone without making an appointment.

When he finally calmed down, he explained that he was deathly afraid of doctors because he'd been so poorly treated by those his previous family had taken him to. He made her promise not to repeat their mistakes.

"I know you think I'm a freak just like they did, but please don't let those mean doctors hurt me again," he pleaded as he climbed into Maude's lap and hugged her.

"Don't be silly. I don't think you're a freak at all," Maude replied returning his hug. "You're the most adorable little boy I've ever met."

"Even though I'm growing too fast?" He asked. "I'll stop eating...I'll do whatever you ask. Just don't send me away."

"Now you really are being a silly boy," Maude replied. "Who's to say what normal is, anyway. You eat as much as you like as often as you like. In fact, I think it's time for a dish of ice cream. What do you say?"

Val nodded as he wiped away the tears. "Chocolate?"

"Sure, chocolate, vanilla, or strawberry. I have all three." There was no more mention after that of his rapid growth.

4

THE DUST COVERED ELLIPSOID shaped object lay in the corner of the cave looking much like the other rocks around it. Shortly after Aeo had sent Val away to meet his new family, the artificial intelligence had cleaned up the cave, hiding the cocoon and FreeForm container in its deepest recesses, then tucked itself among a heap of rocks in standby mode to conserve energy. It would awaken instantly if any threats appeared in the area, but otherwise, it would hibernate much like the cave's former occupant.

It lay there just barely conscious...until two years to the day that Val had left, it started pulsating with a bluish purple glow. It was time to return to work. It switched on the beacon to call the now grown Val back to the cave.

5

VAL STOOD AT THE CREST of the hill gazing down at the mouth of the cave that had been his birthplace. The buzzing in his ears that had continued to grow in intensity over the past two weeks was now just barely perceptible, but he knew if he turned around and tried to leave the buzzing would return.

It had taken a few days to tie up loose ends at Maude's, eliminating all signs of his presence. It hadn't been difficult. He started by suffocating her with a pillow in the middle of the night right after the weekly grocery delivery. That gave him seven days to clean up and get out of town before the young delivery boy would return to notice the front door cracked open, discover her body, and assume she'd died quietly in her sleep.

He adjusted the empty backpack that was a replica of the one he'd dreamt about for the past week, carefully made his way down the rocky slope and into the cave where he found Aeo sitting next to the cocoon and container of FreeForm pupae.

It was finally time to resume the Primary Directive. In the nearby meadow, a sudden breeze blew hundreds of dandelion seeds into the air.

Bonus Content
FreeForm Resumed
Book 3 of the Saga of the
Dandelion Expansion Series

Enjoy these sample chapters

Outside Fallujah

The vibration and rocking of the helicopter combined with the moonless night sky to lull Sergeant Todd John Jacobs into a semi-trance. So much had happened in the past six months since graduating from Ranger school, most of which he still didn't fully understand. The mysterious man who'd met him as he left the graduation stage turned out to be Lieutenant Phillip Ackerson, or Jersey as he preferred to be called. Jersey, an Army officer assigned to special duty with the CIA, had all but hogtied him. He claimed he was there to offer Todd his next assignment per their commander in chief, the President of the United States. That assignment had turned out to be six more months of rigorous training and intel briefings that had eventually led to tonight's mission somewhere in the vicinity of Fallujah, Iraq.

He shook himself awake as he heard the order on his headset, "Five minutes till drop off. Get ready." As Todd looked around, he could just make out James, the pilot, and his co-pilot whose name Todd couldn't remember in front with the crew chief and a door gunner seated behind them. Farther to his right, he saw the outline of Jersey. He knew the other two men assigned to the mission were seated behind the Lieutenant on the opposite side of the helicopter. Jasper Mullins was a good ol' boy from the south so Todd found they had a natural affinity for each other. He found the shorter man, Dewey Stalins more abrasive and eager to start a fight so he'd made it a point to stay out of Dewey's way.

Todd rubbed the smooth metal of his M4 weapon sitting in his lap. He found it comforting and hoped the silencer would allow them an easy in and out if he ended up needing to use it. The weight of the backpack on his shoulders meant it was time for action—the part of military life he loved. Jersey reached over and gave a thumbs up. Todd returned the gesture. The second the aircraft hit the ground they would be running.

Todd felt the aircraft flare, settle and the doors opened. He jumped out into the pitch blackness of a moonless night, ran about fifty feet and dropped to the ground. The helicopter departed without ever coming to a full stop. Todd stood up, adjusting his night vision goggles even though he didn't really need them and looked around. It was important to play the role that he was just like the other soldiers. Three other figures also stood up. The one nearest to him pointed in a direction to the south and started off in a fast jog. The other two moved to his sides and matched stride, with Todd taking up the rear. They ran like this for what Todd calculated to be three-quarters of a mile, putting them a quarter mile from the village that was just over the rise in front of them.

Jersey, in the lead, signaled to stop and kneeled. Todd, Jasper, and Dewey caught up and kneeled beside him. "Damn, this is getting harder every mission," Jersey whispered even though he didn't appear to be at all winded. "I need to get out of this business. All right guys, you know the drill. Refresh if needed and check your weapons and gear. Let's get in there as planned, snatch the package, and get out without anyone knowing what hit them. Any questions?"

Todd looked around. No one had any. Jersey nodded and moved off in the direction of the village. Everyone else moved up to a line position and spread out. As they got closer, Todd could see the wall around the small village and the doorway of the building they were to go through. According to their intel, the door would be unlocked for them, and someone would lead them to the location of the package.

As the team approached the building, Todd noticed some lights in the distance to the west of their position but decided they were probably just goat herders. As he drew nearer to their target, he started having tremors of an odd, yet vaguely familiar feeling which grew stronger the closer he got to the building. What the hell was going on? He'd never felt anything like this on his previous training missions. Maybe those lights weren't goat herders after all.

The creaking of the door cut through the silence of the night as Jersey pushed it open, but before he could enter through it, a man dressed in traditional Arab garb stepped out from the darkness and started firing, hitting Jersey and Dewey. Todd jumped forward and struck the man in the head with the butt of his gun. He yelled for Jasper to secure the area and bolted through the door. Sensing two men on the other side of the door, he cut them both down before they had a chance to react.

Todd paused a moment leaning against one wall, allowing his heightened senses to scan the area. Detecting no one else close by, he signaled for Jasper to bring in their fallen team members. Glancing at Dewey's bloody pulp of a head, Todd knew he couldn't be helped. He started to to turn his attention to Jersey who'd been hit in the side, but Jasper was already apply pressure to the wound. Todd grabbed the unconscious Arab and slapped his face several times to revive him. The man's eyes shot open. Apparently he'd only been pretending to be unconscious.

Todd forced the barrel of the M4 into the man's mouth. "What the hell happened? Why did you shoot at us?" he screamed. The man glared back, defiantly refusing to talk. "So, that's the way you want to play this?" Todd said between clenched teeth. He yanked the gun barrel from the man's mouth and shot off the big toe of his left foot. The man screamed, his eyes growing wide with pain and fear.

"Let's try that again," Todd said. "Why are you shooting at us? You were supposed to help." The man shook his head and spit at him. Todd shrugged, pointed his weapon at the other foot and shot off the other big toe. The man screamed even louder this time. "Okay, one last chance," Todd said as he pointed the gun at the man's crotch. That did the trick.

"Please, no more. I'll talk...please," the man pleaded with a thick accent. After another moment, he continued. "We got word you were coming. We were ordered to set a trap. Please, I was only following orders."

"That's what they always say," Todd replied. He thought about smacking his captive in the head again, but paused to assess the situation first. "Damn, now what do we do?"

"Todd, we have to get out of here," Jersey answered him from where he was lying on the floor, a pool of blood beginning to form despite Jasper's pressure.

"The hell with that. We haven't completed our mission yet. We're not leaving until we've recovered the package, dead or alive."

"We've obviously been made," Jersey said, wincing in pain. "It's time to scrub the mission."

Todd leaned over him and tore the fabric away from the shoulder of his shirt where the bullet had entered. "It's just a flesh wound. Trust me. I can handle this. It's what I've been made for," Todd said. He turned to Jasper. "Take care of him. Keep pressure on the wound and stay alert. There may be others around. Contact me on the headset if things change."

"Will do," Jasper replied, not questioning Todd's self proclaimed authority.

"This asshole and I are going to take a walk..." He looked down at the man's bloody feet. "Well, I'll walk. He'll crawl."

Todd kicked his captive out the door and to the middle of the compound. "Where is he?" he growled to the man who pointed to a doorway two buildings down the street. "Are you sure?"

The man nodded vigorously.

"Good enough," Todd replied as he brought the butt of the gun down on the man's head. The answer had matched his own assessment. As he slowly approached the building, he felt the strange feeling wash over him again. This time he remembered when he'd felt it before. It had been years ago when, as a young kid, he'd run away from home the first time. It felt almost like déjà vu.

Todd crept up to the door and stopped. His senses detected someone on the other side of the door and several others nearby. He could feel the tenseness in them and could hear their elevated heart rates, all except for the person on the other side of the door who remained, calm but why? No time like the present to find out.

Todd lowered his shoulder and smashed through the door. As he burst into the room, the man sitting by a small fireplace put his hands out to his sides and stood up. "Hello, TJ. Man, how you've grown. I thought I felt you out there, but couldn't believe it at first."

Todd stared at the strange man who somehow felt familiar, but unrecognizable at the same time. The man stood over six feet tall, dressed in a long flowing robe. Todd estimated his age to be in his mid to late forties.

"Ahhh, you don't remember me, do you?"

Todd slowly shook his head.

"Well, we met only briefly at the hunting reserve before the Americans tried to wipe us out." Todd continued to stare at the man, racking his brain in an effort to remember his face. "I have often wondered when another of my brothers would show up," the man continued.

"Your brothers?" Todd asked, a confused look on his face. What in hell was he talking about, and why hadn't anyone bothered to tell him during those hours of briefings that the package might know him?

"Yes." the stranger replied. "Most have been killed or captured, but I've eluded capture. Hopefully others have as well. What are you doing here, anyway?"

"I'm here to bring you in," Todd replied, but even as he said it, his brain was busy sorting out what he'd just heard. The man had just said they'd met at a hunting reserve, and he'd called him TJ. It had been quite a while since anyone had called him by that name, and the only hunting reserve he'd ever been at...Homlin's! Holy shit. This guy must have been one of Homlin's flunkies. The pieces were finally falling into place.

"Nah, how can that be?" the man said. "You're one of us."

"One of us?" Todd repeated, trying out the term in his mouth. He remembered hoping that might be the case years ago, but he'd found out soon enough he hadn't belonged at the hunting reserve. Homlin had been up to no good. Todd still had nightmares from watching Homlin almost kill Pat Vogt, his *father's* girlfriend and his sorta stepmother, before she finally turned around and killed Homlin instead.

"I'm not your brother," Todd finally said. "I don't know what I am, but I do know I'm not one of you. I'm here to do a job, so put your hands behind your head." As the man started to comply, he suddenly moved with incredible speed, reaching inside his robes for something. Todd moved just a quickly, firing a short burst from his M4 into the man's chest. As the man slumped to the floor, a pistol fell from his hand onto the dirt floor.

"You're making a mistake," the man whispered before dying. Todd stood silently in the room still trying to make sense of it all. His senses alerted him to the presence of several people approaching from outside.

Todd silently moved to the wall nearest to the door and waited. A second or two later, a dark skinned man poked his head in through the broken door. "Lenny, are you all right?" he said just before Todd shoved his dagger up through the man's throat and into his brain. He used the dagger handle to hold the man up as he pulled his body into the room. He then stepped into the doorway and shot the two other men waiting there. Todd walked over to the man who'd called him a brother. He grabbed him by his robe and started dragging him back to where he'd left Jersey and Jasper.

As he reached the building where they'd been ambushed, everything went to hell. Guns started firing and men yelled in Arabic outside the wall. "Shit," Todd cursed as he yanked the dead man's body through the door and into the room. "What the hell is going on?" he shouted.

"There are a bunch of crazy Arabs outside in the field firing at us. We can't get out," Jasper yelled as he fired off several rounds from the doorway. *Now I'm getting pissed,* Todd thought. He was growing tired of so many people trying to kill him and his friends. "Hold them off for a few minutes, Todd said. "I have a plan."

"What the hell are you going to do?" Jasper asked.

Todd looked down at Jersey who looked pale and only semi-conscious. "We need to get him to a hospital," he replied. "Call James and get that helicopter back here."

"And if it gets shot down, what do we do then?" Jasper asked as he switched his headset on to contact the helicopter.

"Leave that to me," Todd replied, as he slipped out the back door. Todd looked around and ran to another building against the wall and vaulted to the roof. *I thought I was pissed before. Now I'm really POed,* Todd thought. As he started removing his clothes, his body started changing, looking like a much bulkier and darker version of himself except this one had a nasty set of claws and long teeth. *Let's see how they handle my alter ego,* Todd thought as he leaped to the ground and began running full speed at the flashes of light of the firestorm. Todd ran full speed at the first man, taking his head off with a single vicious swipe, then turned on the second man who looked on in horror.

A short time later, Todd returned to where Jasper and Jersey were held up. "I hear the the helicopter," he said to Jasper. "Get him up and let's get out of here."

"What happened out there? Where are the men that were firing at us?" Jasper asked, as he picked Jersey up.

"Let's just say they won't be giving us any more trouble," Todd replied, as he paused to dig a last remnant of dried blood from his fingernails.

College Days

V al stared down at the two envelopes he'd just pulled from his post office box, one a regular size business letter, the second a larger envelope like those used for legal documents. Strange, he thought. He'd been checking his box for weeks like Aeo had instructed him without ever finding anything inside. He'd seen dozens of other student-aged men and women pull out letters and small packages from their boxes. Aeo insisted he go to the post office at least two or three times per week. "We need your routine to look like all the other students," Aeo had insisted.

"But I'm not even enrolled," Val had pointed out.

"Doesn't matter," Aeo retorted. "No one else need know that. Besides, you are sitting in on some of the classes, aren't you?"

"Yeah," Val admitted. "Not sure why I'm doing that either. I already know everything they're teaching. These young humans are really hard to teach."

"Well, that's to our advantage then," Aeo said. "We're doing all this so when you are accepted to MIT you'll know how to act as a grad student."

Now, the business letter had a return address for MIT in Boston, Mass. He opened it and read the short letter. So, I've been accepted, he thought, just like Aeo predicted. Getting accepted to one of the most prestigious universities in the world was just that easy, huh? He remembered what Aeo had told him numerous times. "You don't have to be a genius. We just need for you to act like one...that and have the credentials to back up the claim." He opened the second, larger letter to find a set of transcripts with his name on them from N. C. State University. Hmm, his GPA was only 3.75. He'd have to ask Aeo about why so low. Why not 4.0. Wouldn't that be more consistent with a genius level student?

He closed the door of the post office box and glanced at his watch. Almost time for work, another dull day of waiting on tables, In his estimation, such a job was hardly what a genius level human would hold, even though, due in large

187

part to his youthful good looks, he earned above average tips especially from the university co-eds. Looking like a young Rudolph Valentino had its advantages. Luckily, no one these days had any idea what the silent screen movie star looked like.

"On the contrary," Aeo had insisted when he'd asked. "Many college students wait on tables as a way of paying their bills so I felt it important for you to learn how to do it as well. Plus, well, I needed you to work on your socialization skills."

"Why? I know how to act like a human being," Val had countered.

"Yes you do," Aeo replied. "Just not one that anyone would want to be around. The primary race on this planet is very much into socialization and relationships. This is particularly true as your climbing up the success ladder. Once you have money and power, those skills aren't nearly as important, but remember, you're starting pretty much on the lowest rung of the ladder. It's paramount that you learn to cooperate and collaborate with humans, at least at first. Our first goal is for you to acquire wealth, power and prestige while at the same time keeping you as much out of the limelight as possible."

"Okay, okay," Val had finally agreed. "Poor student waiting on tables is my role for now."

"Yes, but not for long," Aeo promised. "Remember, we're at a major disadvantage not having the technology crystal. Unfortunately, since your memory of its whereabouts was part of the data lost when the Fail Safe Protocol was compromised, we just need to make do with what we have. At the same time, we don't need for you to spend four years earning a undergraduate degree. I'll handle that part at my end with a little well placed computer hacking. Just keep checking that post office box. You'll see the results soon enough."

And there the results were in his hands: an acceptance letter from MIT and a copy of his transcripts proving he'd graduated from N. C. State. Now to get on with the next stage of the mission—establishing himself as an up and coming engineer and scientist.

A Message from Orrin Jason Bradford
(a.k.a. W. Bradford Swift)

As an Indie Author I know just how important readers are. Without people who enjoy reading, authors are pretty useless. Oh, I know I enjoy the thrill of writing the *next great American novel,* but that's really not enough. I need readers like you who enjoy reading my stories. So, thank you. I sincerely appreciate your taking the time to read *FreeForm Reborn.*

Perhaps you would enjoy some of my other books and stories. If you'd like to stay up to date on new book releases, special discounts, and my occasional giveaways, you can also join my **OJB's Amazingly Awesome Readers Group.** Just go to my author's website and blog:

www.wbradfordswift.com

There's one last thing you could do if you would be so kind. Go to your favorite online bookstore and leave an honest review of *FreeForm Reborn.* Honest reviews are really important to help other readers like you know which books to try next. And thanks for being an amazingly awesome reader.

Orrin Jason Bradford (aka W. Bradford Swift)

Acknowledgments

Writing a book is a labor of love for me as well as being a wonderful way to express my life purpose. It's also something that I could not do alone, so I want to thank some of the people who have contributed to this project. Thanks go to my #1 beta reader, James Stepp. (Yes, there's a real James Stepp as well as the fictional helicopter pilot.) James has become much more than a beta reader, but so far neither of us have come up with a better title for him. Thanks for all the time, effort and great ideas you've contributed. I also want to thank the Orrin Jason Bradford Launch Team members. Currently at 260 members, this team of awesome readers helps keep me inspired to write as well as I am able. Thanks for being part of the team. Last of all I want to thank my two Fiverr gems – Kat and Tracy Cartwright (my book editors) and JesiJayy (my book blurber) who all did an amazing job.

Porpoise Publishing

Flat Rock, NC 28731
www.wbradfordswift.com
Library of Congress Cataloging-in-Publication Data
ISBN: 1-930328435
Electronic: ASIN B01HUFDCZM
FreeForm Reborn/ W. Bradford Swift.
1. Science Fiction 2. Speculative Fiction 3. Technology

Cover design by Victor Habbick ~ www.victorhabbickvisions.co.uk/
Typeset in Book Palatino
Printed in USA
First Edition

Did you love *FreeForm Reborn*? Then you should read *Fantastic Fables of Foster Flat* by Orrin Jason Bradford!

In one mountain town, tall tales are that much taller...

"I've seen a lot in my lifetime. You'd think a small mountain town like Foster Flat would be sleepy and boring. Some better adjectives might be strange, surreal, and magical.

I'm Mimi Rawlins. Born and raised in Foster Flat, I've witnessed more than my share of unbelievable incidents here among the mountains. You may not believe some of these stories, but I'm a reporter. I'll tell it to you straight. And I'll promise you one thing: after listening to these stories, your life will never be the same."

Fantastic Fables of Foster Flat is a collection of suspenseful fantasy tales written in the spirit of Ray Bradbury and The Twilight Zone. Inspired by the Great Smoky Mountains themselves, if you like character-driven stories, southern charm, and twists you won't see coming, you'll love Orrin Jason Bradford's assortment of twisty tales.

Buy *Fantastic Fables* to travel deep into the unique mountain town today!

Read more at www.wbradfordswift.com.

About the Author

Orrin Jason Bradford is the pen name W. Bradford Swift uses for his adult fiction to distinguish it from his nonfiction and young adult novels. An avid reader from childhood, he continues to read and study science fiction and fantasy. As a young man, he promised one day to write his own fiction in gratitude to the many authors who kept him entertained and more or less sane over the years.

Swift is best known for his visionary fiction and nonfiction that "entertain while also enlightening and encouraging the reader to expand their sense of what is possible, and then applying that expanded awareness to their life." He is a graduate of Clarion West in Seattle, WA – a residential workshop for writers of science fiction and fantasy. He lives in the "paradise found" of the Blue Ridge Mountains of North Carolina with his wife, Ann, their daughter, Amber and a menagerie of four-legged family members.

His other speculative fiction includes the six-book mega-series, **Saga of the Dandelion Expansion** which includes the FreeForm trilogy and the Kindred trilogy, *Babble, Fantastic Fables of Foster Flat*, and others.

Read more at www.wbradfordswift.com.

About the Publisher

Porpoise Publishing is the imprint of indie author W. Bradford Swift who also writes under the pen name of Orrin Jason Bradford. It is best known for publishing visionary fiction--stories that entertain while also inspiring readers to imagine greater possibilities for their lives.